BEAUTIFUL
—and DEADLY

The submarine's noisy motor was somehow savagely comforting as it broke the Arctic's pristine stillness. The place where they had broken through the ice extended some seventy meters around, but beyond that there was no open water at all.

A brutal, empty, placid world, Werner thought—a world of exquisite but deathly beauty.

A sudden grating, grinding noise, that could be heard even above the sound of the engine, startled him. The ice pack was shifting. In a few minutes they would be trapped, frozen solid, doomed to die in this icy wasteland.

We will send you a free catalog on request. Any titles not in your local book store can be purchased by mail. Send the price of the book plus 50¢ shipping charge to Leisure Books, P.O. Box 270, Norwalk, Connecticut 06852.

Titles currently in print are available for industrial and sales promotion at reduced rates. Address inquiries to Nordon Publications, Inc., Two Park Avenue, New York, New York 10016, Attention: Premium Sales Department.

GREENLAND PASSAGE

Richard Harper

LEISURE BOOKS 🙰 NEW YORK CITY

"This one's for Jake and Ruben"

A LEISURE BOOK

Published by

Nordon Publications, Inc.
Two Park Avenue
New York, N.Y. 10016

Copyright © 1981 by Richard Harper

All rights reserved
Printed in the United States

ONE

The war was truly lost. Kapitänleutnant Werner Reutemann, sitting in the tiny office of the concrete submarine bunker built deep inside a Norwegian fjord near Bergen, momentarily pondered the utter chaos of a defeated Germany as full realization took its brutal hold.

It was the evening of May 5, 1945, and an SS officer was standing, waiting in the open doorway, his leather greatcoat hanging open to disclose a still immaculate gray uniform, from his polished boots right up to the rakish death's-head cap and the collar insignia of a Standartenführer.

Werner Reutemann knew it was in stark contrast to his own shabby U-boat fatigues, his worn leather jacket and the grayish, moldy, once-white captain's cap that lay on the desk at his elbow. But it was what lay beside the cap that really concerned Werner now, his final orders from the Fatherland.

In|special naval cipher, decoded and addressed to him personally from the High Command, which had retreated to Flensburg on the Baltic, it was dated May 2 and signed by Reichsleiter Martin Bormann. Code name: Operation Iceblink.

Werner still couldn't believe it. Hitler had been killed

leading the fighting in the burning Reich's Chancellery in Berlin just five days ago, and Grand Admiral Dönitz, now head of the state, had ordered the surrender of Germany. Dönitz ordered all of his U-boat commanders, wherever they might be, to surface and turn themselves and their boats over to the Allies. This, along with a confusion of orders for Operation Rainbow in which all U-boats were to be scuttled rather than surrendered, created chaos. And now this, a last assignment for him personally from Bormann, the deputy führer, dated two days after Hitler's death. He was to hold his boat and crew in readiness for an extended voyage, a clandestine operation taking two high ranking Nazi Party members in an escape from Allied hands.

Werner rose slowly, brushing his fingers through his dark, close-cropped hair, hair that was already heavily salted with gray though he was not yet thirty. He faced the SS colonel with cool resignation. "All right, Herr Standartenführer, but this order reads only that once I have my passengers aboard, I'm to proceed westerly along the sixtieth parallel, around the tip of Greenland, and northwest into the Davis Strait. It stops there, Colonel, and we both know there's nothing much in that area of the world but the Arctic Circle."

The SS colonel's thin smile was edged with irony, but he said nothing as boot heels echoed in the corridor outside; then he stepped aside to admit an orderly carrying a tray with two steaming mugs of coffee and a bottle of schnapps. Placing the tray on the desk, the orderly saluted stiffly and retreated, while the colonel laced the coffees with the liquor and handed a mug to Werner. "A toast to the success of your final mission for the Fatherland, Herr Kapitän. Your destination will be brought in sealed orders by the SS general who is escorting the official party. Suffice it to say now that you will supply and equip your boat for an extended arctic voyage. Prosit."

Werner drank, but he still couldn't believe what he was hearing. Who were the passengers, he wondered, and suspected one was Martin Bormann himself, and maybe Goebbels. "But why me, Herr Colonel?" he asked aloud. "Me in particular?"

"I'm afraid it's no special honor, Kapitän Reutemann. Even with your several decorations, your politics have always been suspect. It's just that you are one of the few U-boat commanders left with experience on arctic patrols. Ice Devil Group, wasn't it?"

Werner nodded. "For a few months. But that hardly makes me an expert on the Arctic. Those are dangerous waters under the best of conditions."

"We have thought of that too." The colonel returned his empty mug to the tray. "An arctic expert is on the way from Kiel."

Werner sat down again, draining his own mug. "I hope he got out ahead of the Tommies," he answered wryly. "I heard the British took Kiel yesterday."

The SS officer ignored the sarcasm in Werner's voice, or perhaps missed it altogether. "Can I report that your boat is operational, Herr Kapitän?"

Werner looked up wearily at this youthful, pompous, arrogant son of a bitch. Didn't he know the war was over? And they had lost? No, the SS was an army within an army, fighting a war within a war. Fortunately, he'd seldom had any dealings with them. "Operational, Colonel?" Werner raised a curious brow. "It's just out of dry dock, and new batteries have been installed. And I had it out in the fjord today for a test dive—just before word of the surrender." He smiled grimly. "It didn't leak too badly, so yes, I guess you could say it's operational. But then you don't have to go to sea in her."

"Herr Kapitän—"

"Herr Standartenführer, understand me. It's an old boat; it's been a long war; they're all old boats. Whatever happened to the new ones they kept promising us? The big Walther boats with the hydrogen-peroxide, closed-cycle turbines? That's what you need for a mission like this."

The colonel shook his head. "I can get you one of the new Type XXI boats, Kapitän—untested. It's at Trondheim. Or even a newer model of your own boat. But there's nothing else available."

"Then no thanks. I'll keep this one. I already know her idiosyncrasies. U-boats are like women, Herr Colonel, temperamental, moody, unpredictable. One has to get to know them, to humor them. But I'll need some extra armor on the bridge to protect the snorkel and periscopes from the ice. And extra heaters."

"Of course, the comfort of passengers and crew."

"Comfort has nothing to do with it, Colonel. Crews and passengers aboard U-boats do without comfort. The extra heaters are to keep the periscopes and other vital instruments from freezing up. An arctic voyage, Herr Colonel, even with approaching summer, won't be exactly a stroll through the Vienna Woods."

The SS officer straightened his cap, and his expression hardened. "I have left word with the senior officer in Bergen to give you anything you require first priority. You will be prepared to sail on six hours notice, Herr Kapitän." He saluted stiffly, clicking his heels. "Heil Hitler."

"Hitler's dead," Werner answered dully, not even bothering to get up as the colonel left the bunker office. He had just poured more schnapps into his empty mug and replaced the bottle carefully in the wet ring on the tray when footfalls echoed loudly in the cavernous bunker again, and the colonel returned.

"One more thing, Herr Kapitän Reutemann. Whatever happens, the Reich lives on. We will never really capitulate. We may simply withdraw all German forces here to Norway and fight to the last man—and we are hanging deserters!"

Through the still open door Werner watched the booted greatcoat stomping away to disappear in the stark shadows cast by the small caged bulbs high on the ceiling and walls. These same dim lights reflected dully off the rust-streaked conning tower of his U-boat which lay waiting silently at her berth. An old whore of war, he thought, used and abused, but she had served him well. The other berths were empty, very few boats having returned from their last patrols.

He shook his head regretfully, still refusing to believe any of it. But he knew one thing was true: they *were* hanging deserters. Three had been caught and hanged already right in the next bunker only two nights ago. Hanged summarily and without a formal court-martial. Yet how could you desert a war that was over?

And the thought had occurred to him. In fact, wasn't this what he was being ordered to do now, take his boat and crew and run? There were even rumored plans by other captains to escape south by running the blanket of Allied air and sea cover in the North Atlantic all the way to Argentina. But west along the sixtieth parallel past Greenland, and up into the Davis Strait? With an involuntary shudder, he finished the mug of schnapps.

He started to pour another, but instead he suddenly rose in frustration and despair and smashed the bottle on the concrete floor at his feet. Rumors were flying; all was confusion and madness. But getting drunk wasn't the answer. Not for him. He needed a clear head for what was happening all around him. But what in God's sweet hell was happening? What the shit was this? He picked up the secret cipher, sat down, and crumpled it in his fist. Iceblink! Were they mad? "Verdammter Scheisz!" he swore vehemently. The goddamned war was over. Over!

Stuffing the message in his jacket pocket, he stood up and put on his moldy cap. His loyalty was to Germany and the Kriegsmarine; but they had all trooped together to the Nazi madness and it had destroyed the country. Germany lay in ruins from the Oder to the Rhine, and an almost overwhelming upwelling of sadness and self-pity engulfed him as he thought of his dead family: his brothers Karl and Rolf killed at the front; his parents, wife and children—the whole city of Dresden—fire-bombed out of existence. And now everything overrun by Russian and French and Anglo-American units.

He tried hard to shake off the increasingly morbid mood, but he couldn't. What was left for him?

Maybe he would simply disobey the Iceblink order. Maybe now, for the first time in his naval career, he would defy authority. There, he had allowed the thought to enter his mind, and he let it lie there, undisturbed, ticking away like a time bomb.

But he decided he would still have to ready the boat for a long underwater cruise even if it was only to Argentina.

TWO

Having issued new orders for the boat, Werner Reutemann shaved carefully and changed into a fresh uniform. Then he walked across the compound to his executive officer's quarters where he found Oberleutnant Hans Pohl sitting on his bunk in his blue knit underwear, nursing a bottle of Napoleon brandy while he listened to the latest German newscast on the radio.

Hans offered his captain a drink, but Werner politely declined. "The Britishers are about to land in Kristiansand, K'leu," the exec announced, pouring himself some more brandy. "I was saving this for our victory toast; instead, the Norwegians are celebrating, so we might as well too."

"They have reason to, Hans. They've got their country back. We've lost ours." Werner considered his exec an excellent U-boat officer. He was also a good friend. And reaching out he gently loosened Hans' grip on the bottle and set it aside. "The senior officer has ordered all hands restricted to the compound. He doesn't know what will happen next or when. But the Norwegian underground is coming out everywhere."

Hans looked up in anguish, his usual exuberance and optimism smothered by a worried frown. "What are we going to do, K'leu?"

Werner was studying the stress lines in the young officer's face for any signs of strain or breakdown. Hans Pohl was twenty-four years old, and in spite of a long, hard war he still wore a youthful expression of boyish immaturity that belied his true nature. Only his eyes were old, drained by the seemingly endless pressures of frontline duty. Werner knew his own eyes were but a mirror of his young exec's; for they had all aged far beyond their chronological years—those who had survived. And instead of answering the question, Werner took the deciphered Iceblink order from his pocket, smoothed it out, and handed it to Hans without comment.

Hans Pohl was incredulous. "What does it mean, K'leu? The Arctic! Where is there safety in the Arctic?"

"I don't know, but we must not question the wisdom of the High Command. At least we might avoid a British prison camp or firing squad. I want the boat supplied fully—food, winter clothing, spare parts—and top off her bunkers, including the bilges. I want a full one hundred twenty tons plus. Did Haupmann find the short in the port motor switchboard?"

"Yes, K'leu."

"Good. See to everything now. We're supposed to have first priority. I've already ordered auxiliary heaters installed, and saw-toothed icebreakers on the bow and bridge coaming. They're already removing the cannon from the foredeck, and the ack-ack guns from the wintergarten. I assume since we are no longer at war we won't be shooting at anybody."

Hans was already on his feet and dressing. "But what if they shoot at us?" he asked logically.

"If they even find us, Hans, it won't matter how much

armament we have."

"Then we should remove the torps too?"

"Yes. No," he reconsidered. "No, not the torpedoes. Not yet anyway. I've been ordered to report to the senior officer in town. Maybe we'll know more what this is all about when I get back." He didn't really know why he didn't want the torpedoes removed. Just a hunch, a needling worry at the back of his mind.

Naval headquarters for Werner Reutemann's U-boat flotilla was in a nondescript gray stone building in Bergen, but the office of Manfred Voss, the commandant, was lavishly furnished and thickly carpeted. A large naval battle flag draped the wall behind his desk, and the man himself, though barely five feet seven, bore himself like an admiral. He even spoke with exaggerated gestures of his left hand, as if to somehow compensate both for his lack of stature and for the empty right sleeve tucked and tied neatly at his waist. The numerous decorations on his uniform told the rest of the story.

As Werner saluted and reported in, he saw that they were not alone. And he sensed that the big, balding man in civilian clothes, sitting stiffly in the straight-back chair, was a military officer too, even before they were introduced.

"Kapitänleutnant Reutemann," Voss announced, "Herr Obergruppenführer Wilhelm Henke of the SS."

Werner saluted, and his instant dislike for the man appeared to be mutual. The general nodded but didn't bother to get up or return the salute, or even offer to shake hands. He simply took Werner's measure in a brief, hard glance.

"General Henke is the personal representative from the High Command in Flensburg. He will be the bodyguard and liaison for your two passengers, Kapitän. Is your boat going to be ready?"

"It's being equipped and supplied now, Herr Kommandant. I understand the British are already in Kristiansand."

"Their landing is imminent. Everything is going to hell in a handcart."

"That's the reason for all possible haste," General Henke said. "We don't know exactly how much time we have."

"Or exactly where we're going," Werner added pointedly, looking at the general. "My Iceblink order has me only on a westerly course past Greenland and up into the Davis Strait. There's nothing I know of up there but ice. In fact, Baffin Bay at the head of the strait gives birth to most of the world's icebergs."

"Precisely, Herr Kapitän." General Henke's thick, reddish brows had lowered in a scowl. "Ice. Hence the code name Iceblink, a phenomenon of light in the clouds above ice cliffs beyond the horizon."

"I know about iceblink, Herr General," Werner interrupted. "What I don't know is where we're going."

A quick, brief anger shadowed the general's deep-set, puffy eyes. "Of course, Herr K'leu." His familiar use of the shortened term for the captain's rank now angered Werner. Among his U-boat men it was permissible, even desirable; but for an outsider to presume to use it—especially an SS—was maddening. We're going to get along famously, he thought as the general handed him his sealed orders. "You are taking us to the western ice, Kapitän, the far western ice. Through the Northwest

Passage of the Canadian Archipelago, and out through the Bering Sea to Japan. From there arrangements have been made for surface transport across the Pacific to Argentina."

Werner Reutemann was stunned. The announcement literally staggered him, and for an uncomfortably long moment it rendered him speechless. He stared at the SS general with shock and disbelief. Then he turned to the commandant, but saw by his eyes that the general was deadly serious.

Ripping open the orders, Werner glanced through them quickly, confirming everything; and slowly he found his shock and disbelief giving way to a strange fascination. He looked again at General Henke. "Have you considered the chances of success for such a voyage, Herr Obergruppenführer? Mein Gott, the logistics alone—"

"We have carefully calculated everything, Herr K'leu," the general cut him off. "We know the trip will tax the extreme range of a Type VII U-boat such as yours, but much of it will be running on battery power under the pack ice, and by conservative use of your diesel oil when on the surface—"

"Under the ice, Herr General? Under the ice? You realize you're talking about probing our way for miles beneath a polar pack of unknown thickness? Herr General, on arctic patrols in the Denmark Strait I ducked under the pack ice off the east Greenland coast, and in the Norwegian Sea between Spitzbergen and Bear Island, maybe half a dozen times in all to avoid British ships and aircraft; but even then I only penetrated beneath the pack a few hundred meters at most. I never navigated under it!" He turned back incredulously to the commandant whose iron-hard features had not changed expression.

"No one has, have they?"

"No, Kapitän," Manfred Voss answered softly. "Not to my knowledge. That's why we've got an artic ice expert coming from Kiel." He looked at General Henke. "I just got a coded signal before you came in. Their flight got safely out of Flensburg and they should arrive within the hour."

"Excellent," Henke resumed enthusiastically. He had produced a gold cigarette holder, selected a smoke from a gilded and ornately engraved platinum case, and offered one to Werner and Manfred Voss, both of whom declined. "No? They're American anyway." He graciously accepted a light from Voss, then turned back to Werner and motioned toward a lighted table across the room. "We have British Admiralty charts."

Werner stepped to the table and began examining the maps, and again the absolute ludicrousness of the scheme assailed him. "But these are mostly air navigation charts," he said, turning to the commandant.

"They're all we have," Voss commented apologetically. "They're about all there are. The area is still mostly unknown, unexplored."

"But it can be done," Henke insisted pompously. "You agreed, Herr Kommandant, that such a voyage can be accomplished in a submarine by using natural openings in the ice to take in air and recharge its batteries."

Werner looked at Voss, and though the commandant's expression had not changed, the captain sensed that pressure had been applied, political pressure.

"Yes, Herr Obergruppenführer," Voss answered, "it's theoretically feasible. And I agree that with a well-equipped boat and the right commander, it might be done. Surface ships have made it through the ice of the Northwest

Passage. It's just never been done before in a submarine."

Loosing a cloud of smoke toward the ceiling, General Henke glanced triumphantly at Werner. "And are you the right commander, Herr Kapitän Reutemann?"

Werner met Henke's challenging gaze unflinchingly and even managed to suppress a wry smile. "With all due respect, Herr General, I seem to be all you've got. Now I've got one question for you. Just whose mad scheme was this anyway? Any fool knows the quickest, surest way to Argentina is straight down the Atlantic."

Barely restrained fury flickered again in the general's deep-set, hooded eyes, and his pudgy cheeks turned slightly pink at such unexpected impertinence. "Herr Kapitän Reutemann," Henke breathed with the deathly hiss of a snake, "the plan, so carefully worked out by the High Command, was the personal inspiration of our Führer!"

THREE

"The Führer!" Werner shot back, surprised but determined not to be intimidated. "But the Führer's dead, his body burned in the Reich's Chancellery in Berlin."

"That is true," Henke answered calmly. "But it is still his plan, conceived during his heroic personal defense of the capital only last month. An ingenious escape plan for any surviving Party members of high rank who choose to use it. And two have.

"Oh," he added smugly, "we know of your U-boat people's various schemes to escape the Allies' vengeance by sailing submerged with your snorkels directly to Argentina. And the British and Americans probably know about them too. The Atlantic is already swarming with their ships and aircraft—an impassible barrier, even submerged. But Japan via the Northwest Passage, no one would think of that route. And the distance is about the same."

Of course, Werner thought, just an afternoon stroll through the Vienna Woods, but he said nothing. These SS types had no sense of humor, and he had no wish to be hanged.

Perhaps he had already said too much, and when General Henke excused himself with clicking heels and a stiff-arm salute, leaving them to finalize the details, Werner managed a weak Heil Hitler in return.

When Henke had gone, the commandant poured two brandies and handed one to Werner. "I don't envy you, Kapitän; you tread a very thin line. You'd better sit down. I realize it's a shock on top of everything else that's happening, but you wouldn't have liked the Führer's original proposal any better. He wanted a U-boat to take the shortest route to Japan: north between Greenland and Spitzbergen, straight across the pole!"

"Under the entire ice pack?"

"He had the idea there would be enough open leads even there for a U-boat to draw air and charge its batteries by 'puddle jumping' between them. Wiser heads managed to convince him the openings over the pole wouldn't be close enough together, and that just one miss could trap the boat beneath the pack forever. He settled for the Northwest Passage; at least surface vessels have gotten through that. A Canadian named Larsen made it in a schooner both ways just last year. Of course, it took him two years to do it. You'll have to make it in two months, three at the most."

Time, Werner was thinking, if only there were more time. The utter fascination of actually attempting such a voyage was beginning to grow in him now like wildfire. But without the time to plan adequately, to prepare . . .

"I asked you, Kapitän, to assess your chances realistically. This final assignment has the highest priority; probably the future of a Fourth Reich depends on it."

Werner's eyes and thoughts settled again on the commandant. The last thing Germany needed as far as he was concerned was another thousand-year Reich. "Frankly, Herr Kommandant, I don't think we've got the chance of an iceblink in hell."

"Don't be flippant." Voss poured himself another brandy and offered to refill Werner's, but the captain shook his head.

"Sorry, Herr Kommandant," Werner leaned forward and placed his empty snifter back on the desk. "But it's been a hell of a war. I've taken the boat through a hundred hazards, any one of which should have proved fatal. So I'd say the chances, realistically, are zero. But then again, they've been zero before and here I am."

"You realize that under other circumstances I would have asked for volunteers. But," he shrugged.

Warner stood up. "That's something I must insist on, Herr Kommandant. The crew must be volunteers, or at least only single men, or those who have no family to return to."

Manfred Voss frowned. "Then you consider this merely a suicide mission? You don't think you can take your boat through the Northwest Passage successfully?

"Again I'm being realistic, Herr Kommandant. It's never even been attempted in a submarine, and there's so little time to prepare. Anyway, I'm sure my exec will go— he's single—and my chief engineer. But I'll need a navigator. Schrader isn't the best, and he's married. Wife and children still safe in Hamburg, last he heard. And there'll be special navigational problems at these latitudes."

"All right, I'll get you a new navigator, and you can assemble an unencumbered crew. You won't need a full complement anyway. It won't be a war patrol, and you won't be carrying torpedoes."

The torpedoes. It struck Werner then why he had decided not to unload the torpedoes. "I'll need the torps,

Herr Kommandant. A few anyway. If we do get caught under the ice without a breathing hole, I can always try blasting my way through."

"And probably blow up the boat along with you, Kapitän. But you have a point. All right, but three maximum. One in the stern tube and two stowed under the deck plates. That's all. I've already taken the liberty of ordering your forward torpedo room converted into a private compartment for your two passengers. And General Henke will be going—and your ice expert, if she ever gets here."

Werner's head jerked up. "She? Did you say *she,* Herr Kommandant? The arctic expert is a woman? Sir, I protest!"

"And well you might," Manfred Voss smiled sardonically. "But your protest was anticipated, Kapitän, and already overruled, arctic experts being in even shorter supply than U-boat captains. She, like you, was chosen because she's all we've got."

"But, Herr Kommandant, a woman!"

"She is or was," the commandant continued as if uninterrupted, "a civilian employee at the Kiel Naval Base, a marine biologist, but said to be familiar with the arctic environment. I'm sorry, Reutemann, but—"

They were interrupted by a quick knock and the door opened as a young adjutant saluted and announced, "Frau Brandt has arrived, sir. You said to show her in immediately."

A young woman entered, pushing back the furred hood of an anorak and removing her gloves with a shiver. "Brrr, the cold is brutal out there. I think winter is returning; it looks like it's going to snow." She shook free her long auburn hair and glanced curiously at Werner before settling her gaze on the commandant, who poured her a snifter of brandy which she accepted gratefully.

With her hair tumbled loosely about her shoulders she seemed at ease and, to Werner, impossibly attractive. And also quite as impossible as a passenger on a long and dangerous submarine voyage.

Manfred Voss introduced them, and Werner clicked his heels and bowed slightly. "Frau Brandt."

"Kapitän," she held out a slender hand which Werner found surprisingly firm as he acknowledged it with his own.

"Can I send for something to eat, Frau Brandt?" Voss offered. "You must be hungry after your harrowing journey."

"No, thank you. But some hot coffee would be nice, if you have it."

"Of course." He moved to a small corner table where he poured coffee from a silver urn resting on a warmer. "Kapitän Reutemann?" he offered.

"No thanks." Werner was still casting sidelong glances at the woman. He guessed her age at maybe late twenties. Gott en Himmel, he wondered, were they actually going through with this madness?

"I'm sorry to be so abrupt, Frau Brandt," Voss was saying, "but there's not much time for amenities." He handed her the steaming mug.

"I understand, Herr Kommandant." She took a tentative sip of the coffee then set it down, took off her jacket and folded it over a chair. She wore a dark woolen skirt and a blouse that flattered her figure, and sensible flat-heeled shoes. A typical loyal German hausfrau, Werner was thinking, and wondered about her husband.

"The British are all over the Skagerrak," Frau Brandt

remarked, picking up her coffee again. "We only got through because we use a plane with Royal Air Force markings."

"They've already landed in Kristiansand," Voss said. "Bergen may be next. Were you briefed at all on this mission?"

"Only that we'll be traversing arctic waters in a submarine, and you need someone familiar with the ice."

"But we're not talking about the Norwegian Sea, Frau Brandt," Werner suggested coolly, deciding to put his oar in early. "Or the ice off eastern Greenland or Spitzbergen or Jan Mayen Island. We're talking about the Northwest Passage through the Canadian Archipelago to the Pacific, a trip mostly under the ice. You've been to the far western ice, Frau Brandt?"

Her cool green eyes accepted his challenge calmly, and she nodded. "Banks Island in the western end of the archipelago, Herr Kapitän. A German expedition in '38. We wintered there."

"You must have been very young, Frau Brandt," he taunted her, but his tone mellowed as he watched the color rise in her cheeks.

"I was twenty-three."

"Can you show me on these charts exactly where you wintered?" He motioned to the maps covering the table.

Setting down her coffee mug, she moved beside him to the lighted area around the table. "Here," she pointed, "on the southwest coast. An Eskimo settlement called Sachs Harbour. We never went inland."

"How did you get there? By boat?"

"No, we flew in late in August, then flew out in the spring, April I think. We made scientific studies of the flora and fauna, weather observations, and ice conditions such as thickness, hardness and so on."

"And how thick was the ice, Frau Brandt?" Werner asked, his voice still carrying a hint of sarcasm; but he had to admit his respect was growing in spite of his skepticism.

She met his amused gaze defiantly. "The thickness varied, Herr Kapitän. The pack ice averaged ten or fifteen feet, but bergs caught in the pack extended an estimated sixty to eighty feet below the water surface, sometimes more."

A knock on the door interrupted them as the adjutant opened it, ushering Obergruppenführer Henke into the room, and then closing it behind him.

Without ceremony the SS general announced bluntly, "The official party has arrived safely. I've taken the liberty of putting them in your own quarters at the compound, Herr Kommandant."

"Of course, Herr General," Voss colored slightly.

Henke looked then at Frau Brandt. "I see our ice expert got through safely too—good. All we are missing now is the medical doctor who was to accompany us. His plane went down in the Skagerrak, so we will have to do without his services. By the way," he said to Werner, "I've been to the bunker and seen your boat, Herr Kapitän. It won't do."

Werner stared at him. "What do you mean, Herr General, it won't do?"

"We had in mind one of the newer, larger boats." He looked back at the commandant. "I understand a new type of some fifteen hundred tons is ready for service at Trondheim. Larger compartments, a single huge battery—"

"Herr General," Werner cut in rudely, "a new boat is of course tempting; but weighing it against the familiarity of the crew with the old boat and the lack of proper testing—you yourself have set a timetable we can hardly meet with the boat we have now."

"I'm afraid Reutemann is right, Herr General," Voss added. "Most of the advantages of the new Type XXI are either for comfort or for tactical purposes, neither of which is essential for this trip; and you said yourself there is no time. However, if you wish, Korvettenkapitän Schnee even now has one on its first operational patrol. He was reported off the Faeroes when hostilities ended, and has been ordered to return. If you want to risk waiting for him—"

Henke, clasping his hands behind his back, began pacing nervously. Suddenly he stopped, and his eyes fixed again on Werner. "All right," he agreed reluctantly, "have it your way." He glanced at his watch. "It is almost midnight, so we'd better all go to the compound now. Even Bergen is no longer safe. My staff car is outside."

Then he turned again to Werner. "If you will gather up your charts, Kapitän, and bring them with us. Since there is no time to train a new crew, or to wait for Schnee, we will have to make do with what we have. Because we sail in six hours."

FOUR

"I insist on more time to prepare, Herr Kommandant," Werner pleaded.

"He's right," Manfred Voss told Henke who was standing with his arms folded, glaring down at the charts. "We understand the need for all possible haste, but even using his old boat Reutemann must have at least a minimum of preparation time. The actual route must still be worked out, and there are the technical difficulties of operating beneath the ice. Even the essential modifications to the boat are not yet complete."

There were nine of them now, back in the compound and gathered around the charts, which had been spread out on a lighted table at one end of the officers' mess, with thick clouds of tobacco smoke hanging just under the high ceiling lamps over their heads.

Besides Werner, the SS general, the commandant and Frau Brandt, there were Werner's young exec, Oberleutnant Hans Pohl, and his chief engineer, red-haired Leutnant Horst Wolff, thirty-two years old and the "old" man of the boat with six years U-boat experience, the last two served under Werner.

Across from them was the new navigator Voss had provided, Obersteuermann Karl Axmann, twenty years old and with only one war patrol behind him, but purported to be an excellent navigator—and single. Next to him was Obersteuermann Jürgen Heuser, Werner's second engineer, whose black eyepatch and old dueling scar made him appear more menacing than he was. And beside him was the chief yard engineer, Otto Krauss, who was seeing to the modifications on the boat.

Werner had insisted on everyone's presence for the finalization of plans, but he was still surprised at how many wore side arms to meetings these days. It crossed his mind that if the arguments weren't settled soon, someone might try the method used in the old American West.

"Orders were that the boat be readied for departure on six hours notice, Herr Kommandant," Henke was insisting. "I was assured that it would be ready, and I have given you notice. The official party—"

"And I still assure you, Herr Obergruppenführer." Voss gestured with his good hand in his own plea for patience. "But we were only just now able to assemble a crew. Single men." He glanced down the table toward Werner. "Those who still have family left alive have been eliminated, because on this voyage there will be no return to Germany."

"How much have they been told?" Henke wanted to know, looking around to include the other U-boat officers.

"These men, everything. The rest of the crew only that this is a last dangerous mission for the Fatherland. And the number has been kept to a minimum, thirty-one, including," and he deferred again to Werner, "two torpedo mixers."

The others all stared at him. "Torpedoes?" Henke sputtered. "What do we need torpedoes for?"

"If you should get caught under heavy ice without an open lead, they might be used as a last resort to blast your way out."

"And no one's even mentioned the biggest potential danger, Herren," Horst Wolff added, "the most dreaded by sailors and far worse for us, a fire while we're under the ice. We would have to get to the surface immediately to clear the smoke."

With such sobering thoughts, the general quietly relented. "All right, as long as the forward tubes are reserved for the passengers' personal cargo. Everything else is ready, I hope. We've wasted enough time."

"Everything is ready, Herr General," Voss assured him, ignoring his dark look.

"Your pardon, Herr Kommandant," Oberleutnant Hans Pohl, who was standing next to Werner, spoke up, "but there is one important change in the modification of the boat that will take more time if it is adopted."

"Another change?" Henke growled, but Voss ignored him and nodded wearily for Hans to go on. The modifications already included extra armor on the bridge coaming to form a combined icebreaker and protection for the periscopes and radar gear, as well as guarding the top of the tower itself against a direct confrontation with overhead ice; but on the way over Hans suggested to Werner a possibly safer way of operating a submarine under the pack ice, and the captain had told him to propose it.

"What change, Oberleutnant?" Henke was demanding now. "And how long will it take?"

But Hans was looking at Voss. "To protect us against the overhead ice, why not use skis?"

They all looked at him as if he were joking. "Skis?" the

commandant echoed skeptically.

"Yes, sir. If we rigged a large set of skis upside-down on top of the tower," Hans explained patiently, "then the boat might be propelled along the underside of the ice."

"It won't work, gentlemen," Frau Brandt interrupted him quietly but firmly.

Every man at the table turned to stare at her now, and she flushed with embarrassment under their collective masculine gaze, but she repeated stubbornly, "I'm sorry, but it won't work—it's been tried."

"Who tried it?" Manfred Voss asked her.

"An Englishman named Wilkins in '31. He tried to operate a submarine under the polar ice pack using that very method, inverted skis. But he found the ice isn't smooth on its underside. It's rough and irregular. It just didn't work." She glanced uneasily around the table. "The whole experiment didn't work, and they abandoned it."

"I see," Voss said thoughtfully as a profound silence settled around the table.

Werner Reutemann's respect for this young woman had suddenly grown tenfold. He found himself taking her seriously for the first time. "Then we can forget the skis," he said. "But Hans has a point. We'll just have to stay below the ice and count on the saw-toothed icebreakers we've mounted on either side of the bridge coaming to protect the gear and the tower from inadvertent collisions. That along with the icebreaker on the bow."

"And how great a thickness of ice do you think you can break through safely, Kapitän," Voss wanted to know, "if it comes to that? You won't have a torpedo except for extreme emergencies."

Not surprisingly, Werner and the others found themselves looking again at Frau Brandt.

But she only shook her head. "I don't know. How heavy is your boat?"

"Seven hundred fifty tons," Werner answered.

"Whales have been known to break through six or eight inches of ice with their backs," she said, "but I wouldn't think you could attempt more than a few inches without damaging your vessel. And I'm talking about newly frozen ice. Old ice gets diamond-hard and can slice through steel like an axe through butter."

"Well," Voss said as if to shake off the sudden gloom around the table, "there should be enough open leads so you won't have to break through any ice. Or is it still too early in the year, Frau Brandt?"

"That's hard to say. The polar ice is dangerously unpredictable at any time. It's heaviest in the far west, but it will be later in the season by the time we get there, so more of a melt. But it's dangerous either way. Too early in the spring thaw and open leads will be few and far between, it's true; but too late and the melt will have freed huge mountains of shore ice—pressure ice that drifts around with hanging curtains that extend beneath the waterline for as much as a hundred feet."

"That brings up something else," General Henke noted. "Just what is your estimated time for this voyage, Kapitän Reutemann?"

"It's hard to say, Herr General. So much depends on unfamiliar factors." He leaned over the charts. "We'll have to get across the Norwegian Sea first and safely into the Atlantic, and then past Iceland and around the tip of Greenland." He looked up suddenly at the commandant. "What about the Greenland weather stations?"

"Our German stations have all been captured or

abandoned. There are still several Danish-American outposts, one at Kap Farvel and another up at Thule."

Werner nodded. "We can pick up their weather reports, but we'll have to avoid any contact with them." He returned to the charts, tracing their proposed route for Henke. "Up here through the Davis Strait," his finger paused at Baffin Bay, "we'll turn west into Lancaster Sound and the beginning of the Passage. We'll continue westering just under the seventy-fifth parallel through the Barrow Strait and Viscount Melville Sound, then out through McClure Strait into the Beaufort Sea. From there into the Chukchi Sea and out through the Bering Strait to Japan." He looked over at the general. "How much of it will be surface running through clear water at maybe twelve or fifteen knots, and how much feeling our way submerged at three or four knots, I have no idea. We're estimating two months. We'll have provisions for three."

"The ice is always heavy in McClure Strait," Frau Brandt added," whatever the season. It seems to jam up there, coming down from the pole."

Werner looked at her. "And if we get that far and the passage is blocked solid?"

"There's another route through here," she pointed to it with a slender finger, "down the east coast of Banks Island through the Prince of Wales Strait. It's narrow and shallow, but it should be more free of ice." She looked up at Werner. "But there's something else. Most of the Northwest Passage is through deep water, but west of it the Chukchi Sea and the Bering Strait are very shallow. There won't be much clearance between the ice and the bottom, and there's no way of avoiding those."

"Fortunately, Frau Brandt," Manfred Voss pointed

out, "a U-boat needs very little clearance. It can almost crawl along the bottom if it has to."

"But there's another problem, Herr Kommandant," Karl Axmann, the new navigator, spoke up. "Navigating under the ice will be difficult at best. We will have to find open leads to surface not only for recharging the air cylinders and batteries, but to get accurate navigational fixes. The magnetic compass will be nearly useless at those latitudes, and even our gyro won't be entirely reliable."

"True, but you can compensate for compass drift as well as converging longitudinal lines." He looked around the table. "I think the threat of the ice itself will be your biggest problem, Herren," he told them. "If the thickness varies as much as Frau Brandt says, then how are you going to tell how deep it goes or where the leads are when you're running blind beneath it?"

There was complete silence around the table for several seconds as they looked helplessly at one another. Then Horst Wolff, Werner's chief engineer, offered his idea. "If the undersurface of the ice is too rough to get close to with inverted skis, then we need some means of staying away from it altogether, right?"

The others nodded, wondering what he was getting at.

"Well, we use our fathometer to keep our distance off the bottom; so instead of skis why not rig a fathometer upside down and use the same echo-sounding principle to keep our distance from the ice above us?"

"An inverted fathometer?" Manfred Voss tugged a moment at his chin, then glanced provocatively at Werner. "What do you think?"

"It ought to work, Herr Kommandant. Yes, dammit," he added with sudden enthusiasm, "it's just what we need.

It should also help to find leads of open water; the echoes would be heavier against solid ice." He glanced uncertainly at General Henke. "But we'll need time to install it. It could mean the difference between success and failure, life and death."

Henke's brow set in a deep scowl. "How much time?"

Werner looked questioningly over at Otto Krauss, the yard engineer.

Suddenly the focus of attention, Krauss stammered uncertainly, shaking his head. "I don't know—so many changes, Herr Kapitän—I don't see—" he caught the commandant's fierce look and didn't know where to turn.

Voss was leaning forward over the table. "Well, Krauss, can you do it, man?"

"Of course, Herr Kommandant. But if we could move the boat to the yard, all these modifications—"

"You have a floating machine shop, Krauss?" Voss demanded.

"Yes, Herr Kommandant."

"Then use it. How long will it take to complete everything?"

"How many men?"

"All you need," Voss told him.

Otto Krauss straightened visibly. "Twenty-four hours, Herr Kommandant."

"Do it in twenty."

"No!" General Henke's voice was adamant as he brought his fist crashing down on the table. "We cannot wait even ten hours!"

"Herr Obergruppenführer," Werner explained patiently, "like the Herr Kommandant says, our biggest hazards will be the ice and our lack of knowledge in these waters. Even with our expert—and I bow to your expertise, Frau

Brandt—we still don't know the true depths in much of these waters, nor even the accurate location of many of the islands. Most of all we just don't know where and how much drift ice we'll encounter. The boat is already equipped with the latest electronic gear, including a small and sensitive new radar, but I think Horst's idea for an inverted fathometer to guide us under the ice is the best modification the boat will carry, an absolute necessity if we are to have any chance at all. And as captain I insist on time to install it."

He had dropped the gauntlet, and the tenseness went around the table like an electric charge. Werner wasn't at all sure how far he dared go. Aboard his boat he was king, but ashore his power was tenuous at best. Voss could have him hanged, but he was determined if they were going through with this impossible voyage, then they were going with every possible means of making it a success.

Surprisingly, Henke once again relented. "Very well," he mumbled irritably, "if there's no other solution. But this is the final delay." He looked at his watch. "It is now almost 0400 hours. We sail in twenty hours—at midnight—inverted fathometer or no. And something else just as important, Kapitän," the general added, "be sure your fuel tanks are filled to maximum capacity. There won't be any refueling depots between here and Japan."

"I'm painfully aware of that fact, Herr General, but if I might ask you one more thing. Suppose by the time we get there, our bunkers emptied, our supplies exhausted, Japan has surrendered too?"

A profound silence settled around the table again, until Henke growled angrily, "The Japanese will never surrender, Kapitän Reutemann. They are fanatics. They will die

34

on their beaches in banzai charges, but they will never surrender."

FIVE

Still not used to the lifting of the blackout restrictions, Werner Reutemann stood uneasily in the wide pool of yellow light that flooded the steps outside the officers' mess and conferred briefly with his lieutenants. Then he sent them on their separate ways with his final instructions on their preparations for departure.

He had turned up his jacket collar and was about to leave himself when he noticed Frau Brandt standing alone in the shadow of the doorway. "May I see you to your quarters, Frau Brandt?" he offered.

"No thank you, Kapitän. But you might join me. I want to walk awhile in this beautiful Norwegian night." She had pulled up the furred hood of her anorak against the light rain that had turned into a spitting snow which came rushing silently out of the cloudy, moonless dark. "I'll be closed up soon enough in that iron tube of yours," she added, taking his arm. "I've never been aboard a U-boat before and I confess I'm a little leery."

"Nothing to be leery of," he reassured her, "though I'll admit some people refer to them as iron coffins." She seemed somehow smaller, more helpless and feminine outdoors than she had inside. "They're really just a lot of delicately balanced machinery built to move under the sea as well as on it. I'm afraid we're all restricted to the compound now, so we can't walk far, but I'd be glad to show you through the boat if you'd like."

"Is there time?"

"More now than later. Once we're underway, I'll be even busier."

Turning, they crossed the compound to the bunker entrance and walked down the long, narrow corridor which opened into a huge vaulted chamber. Bright floodlights had been mounted over the boat which now glowed with a fresh coat of arctic camouflage, dazzle-striped diagonals of gray and white and washed-out blue. The gun on the foredeck had been removed, and the floating machine shop was being moored alongside while workmen swarmed noisily over her deck and superstructure, the sounds amplified and echoing around the concrete cavern. The sparks from welding and cutting torches reflected off the water.

Long hoses snaked out from the bow and stern ends, and sailors loaded supplies through the open hatches as both food and fuel were taken aboard simultaneously to save time.

Noting the swell of the saddle tanks flanking the hull, Frau Brandt commented, "Your boat has a rounded hull, Kapitän. That can be a distinct advantage in the ice. Seal hunters on Jan Mayen Island use round-hulled boats. If they're caught in heavy ice, it tends to lift them rather than crush them."

Werner smiled. "We're going to do our best not to get caught in the ice, Frau Brandt," he said as they crossed over the gangplank onto the deck, and he helped her up the tower ladder to the bridge where Horst Wolff and the yard engineer were overseeing the rigging of the inverted fathometer.

"It will work, K'leu," Horst said, smiling confidently through his thick red beard.

Werner looked at his chief. "It better," was all he said, then he turned to Frau Brandt. "I'm going to show our arctic expert through the boat, Chief." Horst nodded as he moved aside so the captain could help her down the hatch.

Descending the ladder past the helm and periscopes in the tower, they climbed on down through the lower hatch and into the dimly-lit control room where he watched her uneasy reaction to the mass of instruments around them: the pipes and valves and levers, the gauges and wheels, all a confusing and somewhat frightening maze to the uninitiated. There were even crates of potatoes and cases of eggs still stacked by the chart table, waiting to be stowed aft.

"This is the heart and brain of the boat, Frau Brandt," he said, pointing. "The big wheels control the diving planes, bow and stern; the small wheels and levers and valves operate the vents of the hydraulic manifold to regulate flooding and blowing." He smiled at her look of anxious concern. "It all seems very complicated, and it is. But when it's done in exact sequence by a well-trained crew, the boat responds beautifully. These," he kicked one of the wooden crates, "will of course be stowed out of the way. You want to see the rest?"

She nodded, fascinated. "Of course."

He guided her towards the stern first, ducking through the circular hatch into a narrow corridor that opened on the petty officers' mess, with a lavatory on one side and on the other a small galley where a pot of coffee sat warming on the stove. "It's not quite the elegance of the old Tirpitz or Graf Spee, Frau Brandt, but it's adequate for our purpose—like the coffee." He poured her a mug and watched her sip it. "And you get used to the smells." He was referring to the miasma of stale sweat and diesel oil and cooking odors that permeated the interior.

The boat had been thoroughly cleaned and ventilated, but you never got completely rid of U-boat stench, and he guided her on through another hatchway and along a railed gangway between two massive diesels, and then into the electric motor room. "The diesels are a little noisy when we're running on the surface," he explained, "but submerged, the dynamotors are a quiet, almost soothing contrast. The storage batteries are under the deck plates."

As they stepped through the last hatchway, they were in the stern torpedo room where double sets of three-tiered bunks lined both bulkheads. The chains that usually held gleaming torpedoes were empty. "There's not much room anywhere, is there?" she commented.

"That's why the crew makes multiple use of the same bunks, sleeping in shifts. It's called hot bunking." He smiled at her obvious discomfort. "Don't worry, you'll have private accommodations—my own. I'll share with Hans, my exec. I'm afraid General Henke will have to hot bunk with Horst, my chief."

Guiding her back along the narrow aisle to the control room again, he led her through the forward hatchway which opened into the combination wardroom, radio compartment and officers' quarters. A small lavatory was located here too, and he pointed to a sign on the inside of the door. "The flushing instruction, Frau Brandt. Follow them explicitly, step by step, or you could drown us all." And this time he was only half joking. "As for other sanitary facilities, I'm afraid there's no shower aboard a U-boat. A bucket of soapy water will be the best you can do. But don't worry about it. A week at sea and we will all smell alike."

Pulling aside the green curtain that closed off his own Spartan compartment, he disclosed a bunk with a leather mattress and a sideboard, and a bulkhead with the only oak paneling on the boat. Beside it was a metal locker and a small washstand that converted into a desk. "This will be your quarters, Frau Brandt."

She looked at him. "but I don't want to take yours, Kapitän."

"No problem. I never get much sleep on a voyage anyway. And I doubt this one will be any different in that respect. And like I said, I'll be sharing Hans's bunk."

As they moved on forward through another hatch and through the chief petty officers' mess, they found several men still working on the alterations for the passengers. "That's the forward torpedo room," Werner explained, pointing, "minus any torpedoes now. It's being redecorated to accommodate our guests." But even he was surprised when he peered inside.

A plush red carpet had been installed over the deck plates, and heavy gray drapes lined the bulkheads. A large portrait of Frederick the Great hung over one of the bunks. Expensive looking Turkish tapestries covered the hatches of the four torpedo tubes, and except for the overhead pipes, practically all resemblance to a cramped U-boat quarters had been effectively removed, as if to disguise the nautical reality. In fact, one could almost imagine a wide picture window behind those drapes, overlooking high Alpine peaks.

As they returned along the center aisle to the control room, Frau Brandt asked, "Have you been told who the passengers will be?"

"No, and I haven't asked. I guess I don't really care."

Climbing back up the tower ladder and through the upper hatch, they paused a moment in the horseshoe of the bridge, then walked back onto the railed platform of the wintergarten that had once supported the bristling antiaircraft battery. Here Werner asked Horst Wolff if they were going to make the general's new deadline.

The chief nodded, smiling. "Looks like it, K'leu. Herr Henke won't have anything to yell at you about this time." And then he too asked the question, "Do we know yet who our guests will be?"

"No, Horst, and I don't think we want to know. And by the way, who ordered the arctic camouflage on the boat?"

"The Herr Kommandant, who else?"

Werner smiled wistfully. "That's nice of him, but I doubt we'll be in much danger of meeting any enemies north of the Arctic Circle, and to even get there we'll be traveling mostly submerged."

Climbing back down to the deck, he and Frau Brandt left the boat across the gangplank and then the noisy bunker via the long, narrow corridor. Outside again, the brief snowfall had reverted to a drizzling rain, and they walked slowly beside the sea wall that overlooked the high steep cliffs on the opposite side of the fjord. A half-moon was showing now, slipping in and out among scudding clouds and laying a pale, chilling path across the dark waters. Up on the hill the lights of the town shown brightly after the years of wartime blackouts. It made Werner feel uncomfortably ill at ease.

Then Frau Brandt stopped suddenly and turned to him. "You've ordered that only men without families be allowed on this voyage, Kapitän, does that include you?"

"Yes, Frau Brandt." They were standing so close that

41

he caught the faint aroma of perfume in her hair. "I have no family. A brother was with Rommel's Afrika Korps; killed at Tobruk. Another one died at Stalingrad. The rest of my family lived in Dresden—parents, wife, two children—all incinerated in the firebombing." He found a lump still rose in his throat when he thought about it.

"What about your husband," he asked, "and children?"

She was staring reflectively out over the moonlit fjord. "My Günther was a naval officer too; a lieutenant. He went down two years ago on the Scharnhorst. That's when I was moved to Kiel. We had no children. My mother's dead and I never knew my father." She looked back at him. "So you see, I qualify too."

They continued to talk quietly, and she learned that he had been in and out of the Kiel Naval Base a half dozen times, yet they had never met. His father had served on U-boats in World War I, and he had run away to sea himself at seventeen.

The outbreak of the war in '39 had found him, at twenty-three, a first mate aboard a schooner plying the Baltic. He had entered officers' training and graduated from the naval academy at Flensburg. Assigned as an ensign aboard a mine sweeper in the North Sea, he had transferred to a U-boat flotilla at Kiel. After the fall of France he'd been sent to the U-boat base at Saint Nazaire on the Bay of Biscay.

Promoted to lieutenant, he was assigned as navigator on his first war patrol. And more than a dozen patrols later he was promoted and assigned as executive officer aboard his second U-boat. Then, being one of ten survivors after the boat was bombed coming into port, he was given his own command as Kapitänleutnant and served for awhile with Ice Devil Group out of Tromsö,

Norway, before returning to St. Nazaire. After the Normandy invasion closed all the U-boat bases on the French coast, he was returned to Norway.

The sea had been his occupation, not the war. But the war had come, and for Werner Reutemann the sea had been the place to serve the Fatherland best.

They stood there in the silence for awhile. The rain had stopped and the fresh night wind was raw with the smells of tar and salt and seaweed. Unaccountably he wanted suddenly more than anything else for this young woman beside him to live, to survive. It was inexplicably important to him, and he told her quietly, earnestly, "Don't go with us, Frau Brandt. I mean it; not because you're a woman—your competence is unquestioned—but this mission is suicide. Leave here tonight—now. I can get you out of the compound, and it will be too late for them to hunt for you."

She stared at him in mildly shocked surprise. "And what about you, Kapitän? Why don't you flee too if you think it's suicide? Surely you're not still ready to die for the Fatherland."

"I still believe in Germany, Frau Brandt. My loyalty is to my country and the Kriegsmarine, but I'll take the blame too for looking the other way while a gang of lunatics destroyed it. No, I'm not going to die for the Fatherland; it's too late for that. The war is over. Lost. It is my shame. And my chance to do anything about it is long past. The Fatherland will survive somehow without me."

"Then why are you going on this suicide mission?"

"I'm just curious, I guess—no, fascinated by the challenge." And he was. He knew it now as surely as if a glove had been hurled in his face. Somehow it helped to fill the void of losing the war, and putting it into words only made it more real, a physical, geographical challenge to himself and the boat. "I have nothing more to lose," he told her. "And you know, Frau Brandt, we just might make it. It just might be possible to transit the Northwest Passage in a submarine."

"But not without your Arctic expert, Herr Kapitän," she chided him. "I have no more to lose either, and for me too it is a challenge—almost like going home—because our route goes right past Banks Island."

They continued their walk, and from a nearby barracks the wind brought them the muffled voices of the U-boat men singing the rousing, defiant strains of *Deutschland Über Alles,* though with a stringent note of ironic bitterness.

From the next barracks the songs were more ribald, and there were the distinct shrill sounds of feminine laughter. Frau Brandt looked up at him. "Women in the barracks, Kapitän? Isn't that against regulations?"

"Yes to both your questions. But the war is over." And they walked on, leaving the stone jetty and turning back toward the compound's headquarters where she had been assigned a room.

"You know, Kapitän, that our Führer didn't really die gloriously defending Berlin, don't you?" she asked him.

He stopped and looked at her. "What do you mean?"

"He committed suicide, he and Eva Braun. They were married and then they killed themselves in the Reichsführer bunker after making a will and appointing a successor. Their bodies were doused with gasoline and burned in the Chancellery garden. I got the news before I left Kiel."

Somehow, Werner wasn't surprised. And as they

approached the headquarters' building they saw a German staff car pull into the lighted area around the main gate. It paused only briefly, then was passed by the guards and came roaring inside to brake in front of headquarters. Several dark figures emerged and hurried up the steps and inside where a light still burned in the commandant's offices.

Werner glanced at the luminous dial of his watch. "We sail in a matter of hours, Frau Brandt. You'd better get some rest."

"Inga," she said quietly. "My name is Inga. Will you see me to my room, Kapitän? It's around to the rear."

He walked her to the back of the building and up the stairs. In the dark hallway he waited while she unlocked her door and turned on a shaded lamp just inside. In the pale yellow glow she looked softly radiant. How long had it been now, he thought, since he'd known the warmth and comfort of such a woman as this? How long would it be before— He reached out and gently brushed her hair back from her cheek. "Inga," he whispered.

"I suppose you want to come in, Kapitan," she said softly.

He hesitated, sorely tempted. Then he withdrew his hand reluctantly and stepped back, bowing slightly, stiffly. "No, I'm sorry, Frau Brandt, but there is much to do before we sail. I hope your quarters are comfortable."

He left the building still sweating, striding briskly down the steps and into the cold Norwegian night.

SIX

A few minutes after midnight, in the first hour of May 8, 1945, just two days after General Eisenhower had accepted the formal surrender of the Third Reich from General Jodl at Reims, France, and one day before Nazi forces in Norway surrendered, a German submarine in freshly coated dazzle-stripes of arctic camouflage backed noiselessly on her electric motors out of a hidden concrete bunker near Bergen. Turning, she flooded down to her deck gratings and, with only her tower exposed, began silently navigating the dark tricky waters of the fjord.

An hour later, as the steep cliffs and majestic mountains receded in the darkness behind her, she stuck her bow into the cold Norwegian Sea and slipped furtively beneath the waves.

Operation Iceblink had begun.

Earlier, at quayside, after seeing a somewhat cool and distant Inga Brandt to his curtained quarters, Werner Reutemann had returned to the bridge where he had waited with Hans, his exec, leaning on the coaming and watching as Kommandant Manfred Voss appeared, personally escorting a work party that was carrying eight apparently heavy metal-banded wooden crates, which General Henke had said would be the official party's personal belongings and were to be stowed in the empty forward torpedo tubes.

Henke himself emerged from the open hatch on the fore deck and saluted Voss. As the first crate was brought on board Voss had it set down in front of him and with a borrowed crowbar opened one end himself and offered the general a look inside. Henke, after examining the contents, nodded and stepped back while Voss resecured the crate and motioned the sailors to move it below. He then offered the same inspection for the second crate, but Henke, evidently in even more of a hurry then ever, shook his head, and the remaining seven crates soon vanished through the forward hatch along with the first.

Moments later the official party boarded, both of them unrecognizable in their thick woolen caps and mufflers, with the fur-trimmed collars of their heavy greatcoats turned up. General Henke escorted them silently across the gangplank and along the wooden casing of the foredeck where they too disappeared down the hatch, the general along with them.

Werner had looked curiously at his exec and frowned. "Did you notice anything peculiar about our guests, Hans?"

"Only that one of them had an odd, limping gait, K'leu."

"Yes, that too. But I thought the other one—the smaller—had the distinctive movements of a woman."

Twnety-four hours later, surfacing in the rough waters of the Norwegian Sea and driving through the darkness on her noisy diesels, Werner's U-boat was sixty miles northeast of the Shetlands and hammering westward toward the Atlantic at her top speed of eighteen knots.

The captain was again on the bridge with the spray in his face, but with the SS general beside him at the coaming instead of his exec, who was in the control room below. And as the four lookouts scanned the night around them through powerful Zeiss binoculars, and as the slowly rotating antenna of the radar search receiver beside them hummed with faint impulses warning of the probing radar of distant craft, Werner stared ahead over the foaming bow.

He was remembering that this was the same route the ancient Vikings sailed on their voyages to the New World. However, the Vikings, having touched the tip of Greenland, turned south to Newfoundland while he would be turning north west into the Davis Strait and driving for the Arctic Circle and the Canadian Archipelago and—incredibly—Japan.

"All is well, Herr K'leu!" Henke shouted above the roaring diesels, clapping his gloved hands together and then gripping the wet steel coaming. "Our guests are settled in your forward torpedo room and appear quite comfortable!"

"That's good news, Herr General, but I'm sorry I won't be able to guarantee their continued comfort!"

"What do you mean?"

Werner had raised his own glasses and was focusing them on the darkness ahead. "We'll have to submerge before daylight, which already comes early at this latitude. And if the seas aren't too rough, we'll raise the snorkel and continue on diesel power, keeping the batteries at full charge. But we have a long and difficult voyage ahead of us. I hope they understand this. If not," he lowered the binoculars and looked at Henke as he wiped the spray from the lenses, "if not, Herr General, then it will be up to you to make them understand it. I'll have enough problems with the boat and the ice. It'll be up to you to see that I don't have any with our guests." Even in the darkness he could see the anger and resentment rising like a tide on the SS general's face.

"You dare to—you realize you're dictating to the highest ranking Party members, Herr Kapitän—"

"We are on a U-boat on the high seas, Herr General," Werner explained loudly and with strained patience. "She's not much, only two hundred fifty feet of declicately balanced steel, but I command her. And all our lives rest on my decisions and mine alone. It's best your guests, whoever they are, understand this. Kommandant Voss was negligent if he didn't explain it to you. Anyway, I'm telling you now. You've set me a task and pointed the way, but it's up to me how best to fulfill it. You may ask or suggest or recommend or plead, but I alone make the decisions aboard this boat."

Obviously flustered, Henke glanced nervously around at the lookouts manning the four points of the compass, and then motioned Werner to accompany him back into the railed well of the wintergarten abaft the bridge where they could be sure of not being overheard. "Herr Kapitän Reutemann, I of course recognize your power of command over your ship at sea, but I think you too must recognize just who it is you are transporting to safety!" He glanced back toward the bridge as if still afraid of being overheard in spite of the thundering diesels. Then he moved his mouth closer to Werner's ear. "Our beloved Führer and his Eva did not die in Berlin!"

Werner drew back in surprise. "No? First it was officially announced that he died heroically defending the capital. Then I heard unofficially that they both committed suicide. Now you tell me they live. What am I to believe?"

"Ach," the general's rare smile exposed a gold tooth, "the first was necessary propaganda; the second an elaborate ruse to get them out of Germany. And they are both at this very moment in your forward torpedo room!"

Werner Reutemann said nothing. The faint suspicion had of course occurred to him when he first saw the orders for Iceblink, but he had dismissed it as absurd. Even Inga Brandt's conflicting report of their suicides had not aroused his suspicions until he had watched the two guests board and seen the odd walk of one and the feminine movements of the other. He had seen the Führer only once, when Hitler had personally reviewed the flotilla at Wilhelmshaven, but he had noticed the same trait then. He stared now at Henke. "What about the identification of the burned bodies in the Chancellery and forensic records?"

"Records can be forged too, Herr K'leu. It has all been arranged. The Führer even had the foresight to have a set of old dental records identified as his and planted in the National Archives at Washington, D.C. by our agents in America. There they will be conveniently found and matched against the remains burned in the Chancellery. The evidence will be conclusive."

"Then the suicides, the will, the appointment of successors—"

"All part of the Führer's elaborate plan of escape—to survive and build anew a glorious Fourth Reich!"

"And Iceblink is part of the grand plan."

"Of course, the most ingenious part. Who would think of escaping west to Japan under the ice of the Northwest

Passage? Who but our glorious Führer?"

General Henke's colossal conceit was almost ludicrous, and Werner restrained himself from laughing in his face. The incredible absurdity of the scheme was still overpowering when he thought about it. Yet the challenge of it just couldn't be denied either. And it was a challenge he, Werner, had accepted, for himself and his crew. The passengers themselves meant nothing to him. More so now with the knowledge that he carried the one most responsible for the Nazi madness. But it was a knowledge that sat like a cold hard stone in his gut.

"Let us hope, Herr General," he said slowly, "that luck runs with us. But at the risk of repeating myself, the fact remains that of necessity most of our luck I will have to make myself if we are to survive. To do that I alone must command this boat and everyone aboard her. Now you'd better get below. It'll be getting light in the east soon, and we're going to have to dive."

Following Henke to the bridge hatch, Werner called down after him, "If it will make our guests more comfortable, Herr General, you can inform them that once we clear the Faeroes and the British mine fields north of the Hebrides, we should have a clear run to the ice."

SEVEN

In the seventy-two hours since leaving the Norwegian coast, Werner had seen very little of Inga Brandt. Surfacing only in the already brief hours of darkness, the U-boat stabbed her bow into the long Atlantic swell and continued forging westward, schnorkeling just under the water during daylight to avoid possible capture by roaming Allied forces.

He was forced to dive deep only once during the daylight hours to escape a pair of probing British corvettes southeast of the Faeroes, and only once at night when their radar search receiver began humming loudly and the mate called up from below: "Aircraft, bearing two-six-four and closing!" Moments later a flare burst overhead, turning night into day, as they dived into the depths, bracketed by two bombs which slammed the U-boat even deeper and out of control.

The chief engineer had caught her at 220 meters, and other than shattered glass in the dials and leaking oil lines, she had sustained no damage. But Werner brought her up only to a hundred meters and, rigged for silent running, crept along for over two hours while the mate listened on the hydrophones for any further danger.

But no surface vessels converged on their location. The

danger had passed. And all during the ordeal nothing was seen or heard from their guests in the forward torpedo room. General Henke took them a meal on a tray, a vegetarian diet consisting of vegetable soup and a jellied omelet, and reported stiffly that they had sustained no injuries. A little of the color had even returned to the general's face.

Werner then had the boat brought up again to snorkel depth. He spent most of his time in the control room pouring over the charts with Karl Axmann, his new navigator, or in the officers' mess with the chief engineer or his second, Jürgen Heuser.

He managed a catnap occasionally in his exec's bunk, while General Henke and their guests seemed to sleep away as much of the time as they could, which was just as well. But even this wasn't easy when they were snorkeling, a maneuver which had never been one of the more popular aspects of U-boat life, since in any sea at all the snort valve kept snapping open and shut, causing it to suck air first from outside and then from inside the boat. The resulting chronic changes in air pressure were extremely painful to eyes and eardrums, and Henke was soon his old self, complaining loudly about his own discomfort and that of the passengers.

Werner ignored him with a shrug. "Wait till the bread molds and the eggs rot and the hours of constant pitching and yawing make even seasoned sailors giddy, Herr General. I warned you this would be no pleasure cruise."

But remarkably, in spite of the difficulties in adjusting to bouts of seasickness, the frequent snorkeling and the cramped, stale quarters, they had all fallen quickly into the monotony of U-boat routine.

Though nothing had been announced, the word as to

the identity of their passengers had spread through the boat in a matter of hours, and Werner noticed an underlying tenseness among the crew. It was nothing he could establish as fact, just something he sensed, even wondering if he just imagined it. It didn't seem to affect their efficiency in handling the boat. Perhaps it had even sharpened it, and he remarked about it to the chief.

"We're Kriegsmarine, K'leu," the red-haired Horst Wolff had answered simply. "We obey orders."

"Yes," Werner mused aloud, "maybe that's been our problem all along; we have never questioned our orders."

At meal times Henke continued to carry a vegetarian dish to Hitler and Eva in the forward torpedo room. No one but he ever saw them. And even he would return to eat with the officers and Inga Brandt at the fold-out table in the aisle of the wardroom, where the talk was mainly concentrated on the business of their escape.

Inga once asked Henke if Eva knew there was another woman aboard. The general had shrugged. "Why should she care?"

"I just thought that maybe, if she needs anything—"

"She and the Führer are content, Frau Brandt," Henke told her. She had dropped the subject.

For Inga Brandt too the Führer's presence was troublesome knowledge. Wearing a rumpled and oversized set of green U-boat fatigues under a thick blue turtle-neck sweater, she had tied her hair back with a yellow scarf. Already her face was streaked with the traces of oil that seemed to be everywhere and on everything. She had become acclimated to the constant motion of the boat after one bad bout with seasickness, and she felt she might even get used to the smells and the constant need to duck pipes or valves or wheels when moving through the passageways. But the knowledge that they carried the head of the German Reich and his wife as passengers was sitting a little heavy as she studied the face of the captain who had joined her at the table.

She had needed some time alone to adjust, not only to the boat but to the man. Strangely attracted to him from that first day in Kommandant Voss's office, she still wasn't sure she'd have slept with him that first night in Norway if he'd given her the chance. The fact that he hadn't had bruised her ego, but it had also given her time to reflect. Now she was determined not to fall in love with him.

She had had only one serious affair since the death of her husband, and it too had ended tragically. She didn't want another; especially not now, not under these conditions. Still, the magnetism of Werner Reutemann's personality was even stronger now than it had been before.

Now that the others had left, she was watching him covertly over the rim of her coffee mug. He was growing a beard. They all grew beards on these voyages, especially in the colder climates. She knew he must be no older than she was, yet his hair was flecked with gray and the lean, angular lines of his face couldn't quite hide the strain of endless responsibility and command decisions. He had the perpetual squint of a sailor, and his dark eyes seemed haunted by the years of warfare behind him.

For three days and nights he had been busy with the technical difficulties of the voyage, as she knew he would be. Her duties would commence only when they reached the ice. But though she had not deliberately avoided him, it was a rare moment when they actually found themselves with only each other for company. And the memory of their last night in Norway still embarrassed her.

But the larger knowledge of the identity of their passengers had now overwhelmed even this, and she wondered how it had affected him. Leaning forward, she whispered urgently. "You didn't know? About the Führer and his wife?"

Werner shook his head, cupping the steaming mug in both hands as he sipped it. "Not until Henke told me after we were at sea. I guess I suspected, but I really thought it was Bormann and maybe Goebbels or Himmler. I suppose the marriage in the Führerbunker was real, but the suicide pact was a hoax. So we carry the elite, the cream of the Third Reich."

"But what could have happened to Bormann and the others?"

"Goebbels evidently did commit suicide, according to Henke, and killed his wife and children along with himself. The general says Bormann chose another escape route arranged through the Vatican in Rome." He smiled grimly. "It seems the Führer didn't quite trust the Church that much, or was too taken up with his own brash scheme for escape."

"It's unreal." She shook her head, wishing for a cigarette, but smoking was allowed only while surfaced. "Our Fatherland crushed, lost, and we're taking its leader and his wife on a run for the far western ice."

He stared at her. "Why does it bother you, Frau Brandt?" he asked, curious. "You knew they'd be some high-ranking Party members."

"But the Führer himself!" She shuddered involuntarily. "Somehow one of the others—even Reichsleiter Bormann; but the Führer himself when he's supposed to be dead! It's unsettling."

"And pitiful," Werner added. "I don't know about Eva,

but the Führer's health is not up to such a voyage as this, physically or mentally."

They were interrupted by Obersteuermann Axmann, the young navigator, ducking through the hatchway. "Your pardon, Herr K'leu, but it is nearly sunset."

Werner rose, excusing himself as he glanced at his watch. "What's your reckoning of our position, Karl?"

"Passing ten degrees west longitude, a hundred fifty miles southwest of the Faeroes, Herr K'leu. We should be clear of the Englander's mine fields."

Pausing at the chart table in the control room, Werner glanced at the plot, then at the gauges and dials around them. They were running on the electric motors at periscope depth, making four knots, and he called up the tower where the exec was seated at the scope, "Anything in sight, Hans?"

"No, K'leu. Low overcaste and a heavy swell; patches of fog; visibility about a thousand meters."

"We've had the antenna up," Karl said beside him, "but no radio traffic."

Werner glanced at the hydrophone operator whose head was bent intently over his set as he listened.

"Noting on the H.E. either, Herr K'leu," Karl added.

"Surface," Werner ordered. "Let her ride on the vents till we have a good look around." Turning towards the chief who was standing beside the men at the manifold, he watched him signal them and the planesmen seated at their wheels.

As air shrieked into the tanks, the U-boat angled sharply upwards just as General Henke struggled through the forward hatch into the control room, catching himself awkwardly as he stumbled. "What's going on?" he demanded.

"Just surfacing, Herr General," Warner told him, hanging his binoculars around his neck as he started up the tower ladder with the four watchkeepers close behind him. "Come up if you like. But if I order a crash dive, you better not waste any time getting below if you don't want to be left behind." He passed Hans in the tower, then spun the upper hatch wheel, pushing it open amid a whoosh of escaping air.

Out on the open bridge he brought his binoculars to his eyes as the four lookouts went to each quarter of the bridge and did the same. A raw wind stood out of the north-east, and the submarine, still flooded down to her slatted wooden deck casing, rode heavily in the heaving swell. The radar search receiver beside him was silent, and the sea was empty except for the fast disappearing sun, which was a flattened reddish-gold streak caught momentarily between the water and the clouds.

Karl Axmann, coming up to stand beside Werner with his sextant, managed to get a sighting as Werner lowered his glasses and bent over the voicepipe: "Blow her out, Chief, and switch to the port diesel and starboard motor. Half ahead both. We'll conserve fuel and still maintain a full charge."

As the port diesel coughed and started, the chief ordered the exhaust bled into the diving tanks to expel the last remaining water and lift the boat fully to the surface. And as the clutches were engaged and the boat surged forward through the swell, General Henke's balding head appeared in the open hatch. "Is it all clear, Kapitän?" he asked.

Werner glanced down at the general, noting the freshly shaved cheeks. Smiling through his own new growth of beard he nodded, "Safe as a baby in its bath, Herr

Obergruppenführer. Come on up."

The general climbed on out and walked back off the bridge into the wintergarten where he grasped the wet iron railing, braced his feet against the vibrating sway, and gazed fiercely out at the dying day.

"Smoke while you can, Herr General!" Werner called to him over the roaring diesel. "It's allowed only while we're surfaced, and then only in the tower or up here. You want to bring our guests up awhile too?"

Henke looked around and shook his head. "They do not wish to leave their quarters."

Werner shrugged and raised his glasses. It didn't matter. He knew that with the compressors running now, the fresh sea air was being drawn through the entire boat, driving out a little of the clammy, muggy, stinking closeness. But on any voyage, if there was a chance, he liked to let the various crew members come topside at least once in awhile for a look and a smell of the real world. And cupping his hand over the voicepipe again he called down, "Chief! Send up a few of the hands to stretch their legs in the wintergarten, and Frau Brandt too, if she wishes."

But within the hour the weather changed, the wind rising to six on the Beaufort scale as the U-boat bored through green walls of water and wallowed sluggishly in the troughs. Soon they could barely see over the crests of the waves.

And for the next seven hours of stormy darkness, Werner kept the boat on the surface at speeds ranging from twelve to fifteen knots, keeping both the batteries and air cylinders at full charge, and diving at dawn only when the slowly revolving radar search receiver began picking up strong impulses.

When the order rang down on the engine room telegraph, Obermaschinist Günther Hardegen and his mate Jon Müller let out the clutches and shut off the air intake manifold. Wiping his hands on an oily rag, Günther tossed it to Jon and picked up a spanner. They were both braced at the gangway railing between the two massive engines as the boat's bow angled steeply down and the electrical artificers in the next compartment started their generators and replaced the roaring diesels with a constant, soothing, humming sound.

Günther preferred the thundering of his diesels. A brawny bull of a man, he was stripped to the waist in the warm engine room, and his oil-smeared, tattooed arms and chest were matted with coarse black hair. Wearing his cap at a jaunty angle, he was perfectly at home in the noisy vitals of the U-boat, and he had been on this particular boat and with this one captain for the past three years of war.

Single, he had only the sea and the Kriegsmarine, the U-boat and his captain. The fact that he was actually surviving the war was totally unexpected. He had survived a hundred depth-charge attacks, attacks that sometimes lasted for twenty or thirty hours and had them all grinding their teeth and praying for it to end one way or another.

He had only a vague idea of what they were attempting now; but he had no doubt that it could be accomplished. He had more confidence in his K'leu than in God, and he knew the captain's uncanny ability to escape disaster was the only reason they were still alive. It was a lucky boat and a lucky skipper, and he didn't give a shit where they were bound or who they had on board. He had nowhere special to go anyway, or no one to go to. The whores in their old ports of Brest and St. Nazaire, and probably even in Bergen now, were most likely servicing the Yanks.

The rumor that they carried the Führer himself in their forward torpedo room didn't really impress him either, even if it was true. In fact, there was only one thing that did bother him now, and he had mentioned it to Jon. That was having two women on board. Women didn't belong at sea; they were bad luck. He had seen the captain's woman, the ice expert, but not the Führer's; and he knew he probably wouldn't see her, since he seldom went anywhere except his engine room and the crew's quarters in the stern. He seldom went topside, even when it was allowed. When at sea his world was here, beside his pounding diesels in the roaring bowels of the boat; and he still felt the vague, intangible certainty that he would die here, eventually.

In the control room Karl Axmann was bent over the lighted chart table, plotting their course with dividers and a parallel rule. For two more days, running in darkness on the surface and snorkeling through the lengthening daylight with the antenna mounted on the snort mast, they had continued monitoring the radio traffic in the area, until even that diminished as they pushed steadily westward.

They had picked up the thrashing propeller screws of destroyers on the hydrophones, but the ships had passed away to the north, headed for Reykjavik. Werner had finally surfaced again and run on the diesels until nearly dawn when Karl got a couple of star shots through breaks in the clouds and a running fix on their position.

They were snorkeling now, still on the diesels but three meters beneath a relatively calm sea as they passed twenty-five degrees west longitude. If his calculations were correct, Karl knew they were about four hundred miles from a meeting with the first drift ice off the southeast Greenland coast, and he waited impatiently for the captain's order to change course. Karl Axmann had no intention of going to the Arctic.

Relatively new to the U-boat service, he had missed the "good" years, the glorious U-boat victories of '40, '41, and '42. All he had known was defeat. On his single patrol they had sunk no ships, and he had endured with his mates the mind-wrenching depth chargings that had seemed endless at the time, attacks that had numbed his nerves as well as his mind.

Finally, two days after his nineteenth birthday, he had survived his first and last patrol with his boat sunk under him, leaving only himself and the four lookouts alive simply because they had been on the bridge when a corvette had turned sharply out of thick fog and darkness and cut them in two. He had even escaped a British prison camp, and now he had survived the war itself. So he had no intention of dying in the Arctic.

He had tried to get on one of the other boats making clandestine escapes to Argentina, but that plan had failed, and he had volunteered for this last special mission, as Kommandant Voss had put it, certain that it too had to be a stratagem for an escape direct to Argentina. The elaborate plans and special arctic camouflage and gear were just a ruse. But he was beginning to worry.

With Hitler on board they surely weren't really going to try the long icebound route to Japan. Yet he felt too that the war had probably been lost primarily because of the Führer's harebrained schemes, schemes just such as this one, and he was only now beginning to realize that it was entirely possible they would actually remain on this westerly bearing. The whole idea clutched at his gut like a claw. The last chance to swing south was rapidly approaching, yet the captain said nothing.

And for another forty-eight hours the captain continued to say nothing. It was Joachim Lutz, the radio mate, who first reported the scattering of ice on the radar as well as an aircraft approaching. They dived. An hour later Hans Pohl was shouting down from the tower where he was manning the search periscope. "No sign of the aircraft, K'leu, but there's ice! Bearing two-eight-zero; range five thousand meters. Ice ahead!"

Climbing up into the tower, Werner slid onto the periscope seat that Hans had just vacated. Pressing his face to the rubber cup, he twisted the handles and worked the foot pedals as he swung the scope around the horizon. The sky was indeed clear. And there it was ahead: the ice, great, dazzling, white monoliths drifting south and dotting the western horizon.

He had just given the scope back over to Hans and ordered a slight course alteration to give plenty of clearance around the tip of Greenland when General Henke climbed up into the tower. "What's this about ice?"

"We're approaching the southern edge of the drift ice off Greenland," Werner said.

Hans gave Henke a look through the scope as Werner ordered the chief to surface and called down for Inga Brandt, their ice expert.

The U-boat rose, dripping and glistening in the first bright sunlight in days, and drove like a knife over the surface of a flat green sea as they opened the hatch. The bridge and wintergarten became crowded with the watch and several officers and seamen coming up from below, along with Werner and the general and Inga Brandt.

Then Henke, standing by the periscopes behind Werner, who was watching the distant parade of icebergs through his binoculars, moved closer and announced above the roar of the diesels, "The Führer wants to come up now, Herr Kapitän, and see the ice for himself!"

EIGHT

While the dazzle-striped submarine sliced steadily westward through a calm green sea, the two figures huddled in greatcoats and woolen caps climbed awkwardly out of the hatch on the foredeck, assisted by a sailor and General Henke. Up on the bridge Karl Axmann and the four lookouts kept their eyes obediently to their binoculars, but Werner and Inga Brandt, moving to the forward edge of the coaming, managed to look down without appearing to stare.

Eva's face was covered to the eyes with a thick woolen muffler. Werner had never seen her anyway; but he would never forget Adolf Hitler. The Führer's identity was obvious, in spite of having shaved off his mustache. His face had a pasty, pale, unhealthy look as he stepped to the iron railing and braced himself with his right hand against the rolling, vibrating motion of the U-boat. His left arm, hanging at his side, was trembling noticeably.

The sight before them was magnificent. The great white bergs were all around them now, varying in size from small houses to multistoried buildings, and all sailing along on the cold East Greenland Current, their reflected brilliance set against a clear blue sky.

The Führer even said something to Eva, and she

answered briefly. Whatever the exchange was, it was smothered by the thundering diesels. They stayed on deck less than three minutes, turning suddenly from the rail and allowing Henke to escort them below again while the sailor closed and secured the hatch behind them.

Werner, who had been conning the boat from the bridge by calling the frequent course changes down the open hatch to the helmsman in the tower, looked at Inga and shrugged. "I suppose our Führer is satisfied now that we're really on course for the Arctic."

"I don't even think they noticed the awesome beauty of it all," she answered.

"Why should they? To them it's merely an escape route, cold and dangerous and unknown."

Inga shivered, her face framed in the fur-fringed hood of her anorak as she rubbed her mittened hands together. "Just looking at all that ice makes me cold too. But, God, it's a majestic sight!"

Karl Axmann, standing by the periscope standard behind them remarked, "Beautiful indeed, Frau Brandt. But Herr K'leu," he turned to Werner, "now that the Führer has seen the ice, isn't it time we plotted a course south if we're really going to make it to Argentina?"

Werner looked around at his young navigator, his brow arched in sudden surprise. "But Herr Obersteuermann, we are going to make it to Argentina, or at least to Japan, via the Northwest Passage, just like we planned."

For the next thirty-six hours the U-boat held to its westerly course, traveling rapidly on the surface and maneuvering among the ever-increasing bergs and pans of ice through the lengthening hours of daylight until, approaching the southern tip of Greenland, Werner noted the date in his log as they submerged and raised the snort mast to avoid any possible detection by aircraft that might still be operating out of the Danish-American weather station at Kap Farvel.

Once, as the fog lifted momentarily, they sighted the distant, mountainous coast through the periscope. With the antenna attached to the snort, they managed to monitor a local weather report. Joachim Lutz, in the radio compartment which was tucked into a corner of the wardroom, copied the forecast, which wasn't very encouraging.

Late spring storms off the Greenland icecap were delaying the retreat of the pack ice in the Davis Strait, and an arctic gale was even now moving down the west Greenland coast, nearing blizzard conditions, with temperatures in the high twenties and winds gusting to forty knots.

There was also a news broadcast, a delayed communique out of Stockholm about orders for the demobilization and disarmament of all German armed forces to the German High Command in Flensburg from General Eisenhower. There was also a report of tens of thousands of German prisoners already being moved eastward under heavy guard to be put to work rebuilding Soviet cities and factories.

While Henke took this news to Hitler, Werner motioned to Hans Pohl who followed him through the hatch into the control room. A sailor brought them fresh mugs of hot coffee. There he ordered his chief engineer to maintain snort depth and Karl Axmann to continue conning the boat from his position at the periscope in the tower, while he bent over the lighted chart table with Hans at his elbow.

"We'll hold this course and continue snorkeling as long

as the sea remains calm," he told his exec. "I want to be well clear of the Greenland coast before we surface again and turn northwest into the strait."

Hans nodded thoughtfully, sipping at his coffee. "There may still be American air patrols out of Newfoundland that we'll have to avoid too."

"Maybe, but I doubt it now, Hans, with the war officially over. We probably have nothing to fear from the weather stations at Frobisher Bay on Baffin Island either, or the one up here at Thule. They shouldn't be looking for stray German submarines. But you're right, we'll take no chances. We'll keep to the center of the strait all the way to Baffin Bay, or at least until we are forced to submerge by the ice."

Hans's blue eyes met his over their steaming mugs. "Where should we meet it first, K'leu, the ice pack itself, the solid stuff?"

"Probably close to the Arctic Circle, according to Frau Brandt. And that's where our voyage really begins." He looked around at his chief engineer. "We'll have to practice a drill for vertical ascent through the openings in the ice, Chief. Are you ready for it?"

The red-bearded lieutenant grinned confidently. "Ready, K'leu."

Werner looked back at his first officer. "And you, Hans?"

Oberleutnant Hans Pohl nodded enthusiastically. "It's really never been done before, has it? Never in a submarine."

"Never even been tried, except that aborted attempt with skis. It's probably impossible. You know that, don't you?"

"Impossible, K'leu? Like our escape from that British

corvette in the shallows of the Skagerrak a year ago? Or the time you went deeper than any boat's ever gone before to escape those destroyers off the Canaries in '43? You forget, I've been with you through two years of the war. I've seen you overcome the impossible too many times."

Werner smiled warmly. He had always tried to deserve the faith his officers and crew showed in him, but he couldn't help wondering if this time he had bitten off a little too much. "Anyway," he said, "I want to duck under one of these giant bergs first and test the inverted fathometer. If the damn thing doesn't work, we might just have to follow Karl's suggestion and head straight south down the Atlantic for Argentina."

In Werner's curtained nook off the wardroom, Inga Brandt was sitting at the small desk, making some calculations from her notes taken seven years ago when on the expedition to Banks Island in the western archipelago. As the ice expert on this incredible adventure, she had serious doubts as to what they might be in for.

Other than the months at Banks Island, her arctic experience was limited to a surface voyage along the drift ice off the east Greenland coast, and a later land expedition across Spitzbergen. And so much about the Arctic was still unknown to anyone. Much of it wasn't even accurately mapped, especially in the archipelago; yet she felt an almost eerie confidence in Werner Reutemann's abilities with his U-boat. If anyone could take a submarine under the pack ice successfully, it would be him.

And it wasn't just her own feelings about the man. She could see the aura of confidence he generated among the crew, a confidence that was reflected in their performance. She could almost feel it in the U-boat itself; it responded to his touch like a woman. She felt the warmth rise to her cheeks, remembering again their first encounter.

Having seldom had feelings like this since word of her husband's death, she had found it extremely unsettling that first moment she'd walked into headquarters in Bergen and experienced the same sheer physical attraction that had first drawn her to Erik Brandt. Werner Reutemann. She found herself writing his name repeatedly on the margin of her notebook like a silly school girl.

The rattle of the rungs on the green curtain covering the doorway was startling, interrupting her reverie, and she jumped with a guilty reflex as General Wilhelm Henke pushed aside the curtain and looked in.

"Your pardon, Frau Brandt," his voice was tinged with slightly amused contempt, "but there's no door to knock on." His hooded eyes quickly took in the Spartan quarters, the narrow bunk and thin leather mattress, the locker with its flecked gray paint, the single chair and the desk that converted into a washstand. Only the dark oak paneling over the bulkheads gave some relief and warmth to the otherwise cramped and harsh surroundings.

"There's such a thing as calling through the curtain, Herr General," Inga admonished him stiffly. "Your intrusion is unwarranted and resented. I could have been dressing."

"Come, come, Frau Brandt," he said placatingly. "Inga, isn't it? No need for rigorous formalities here, surely." He had stepped inside and let the curtain fall shut behind him. "We're all friends, and it's going to be a long voyage. Certainly you don't consider yourself the exclusive property of Kapitän Reutemann?" He had a sly, oily smile that exposed a gold tooth and turned her stomach. His breath reeked of cognac.

"I'm no one's property, Herr General," she snapped. "And I'm certainly not the ship's whore. Now, I'll thank you to leave. I'm busy."

"Of course, Frau Brandt." He made a mocking bow. "I wouldn't want to intrude on our ice expert. Perhaps another time, my dear, when you're more in the mood."

"Herr General," she spoke in a small, tight voice full of sharp, steel splinters, a tone that caused even a general to pause in the doorway, the curtain half drawn, "there will be no other time. You have your duties and I have mine. They are different and separate and will remain so. Is that understood, Herr General?"

Henke shrugged indifferently. "As you wish, Frau Brandt. Yet we are all social animals, don't you agree? And it's a small boat. I think you'll come around." He let the curtain fall shut between them.

Pig, she thought, clenching her fists and resisting the urge to pound the desk or throw something. She got up and paced the few feet allowable in the tiny compartment. She wished the captain would sleep in his own bunk. Or at least sleep somewhere. He had hardly put his head down in days. How could he go on like this? She knew he was of necessity running the boat as if still on a wartime patrol. But surely once they were out of the Atlantic and heading up into the Davis Strait, the war with the Allies would really be over, and the war with the ice would begin. She sat down again, not daring to wonder if they might lose that too.

"Kapitän to the wardroom!" The note of urgency in the voice on the intercom alarmed her and she rose and pushed aside the curtain just as Werner and Hans ducked through the forward hatchway and into the wardroom. They stopped and stared at where Oberbootsmann Fritz Oder was pointing: the radio compartment.

The radio transceiver had been smashed, destroyed, obviously beyond recovery. She knew there must be spare parts aboard, but certainly nothing to repair such extensive and deliberate damage as this. Werner was looking around at several others who had gathered in the wardroom, including General Henke. "Didn't anyone see anything or hear anything?" He looked past them at Inga who was still peering through the curtain.

She shook her head mutely. And Werner understood. With the steady rumbling noise of the diesels, she couldn't have heard. Probably nobody had, except the culprit. A few well-placed strokes with a hammer or bar. But who? And why? He stared at Fritz Oder who had reported it, but quickly dismissed him. The others, including Henke, could all be suspect.

It was just after noon on the 19th when Werner made an entry in the log and gave the order to surface. Then he climbed out on the bridge with the lookouts and Obersteuermann Karl Axmann, who brought up his sextant and shot the sun and moon both through a cloudy haze and fixed their position.

Finished, the navigator looked glumly at Werner as the captain called the course correction to the helmsman in the tower. "Hard to starboard, Steersmann. Come to bearing three-four-zero."

"Hard to starboard, sir," the helmsman echoed. "Steering three-four-zero."

Karl Axmann, shielding his sextant from the bow spray as the U-boat angled sharply into the wind, said nothing. But he still couldn't believe it. Even now, without radio communications for weather reports and bearings, they were still going to attempt the icebound Northwest Passage to Japan.

NINE

He was skiing high on the slopes of the Zugspitze, exhilarated as he swooped in a slalom down the steep inclines, sweeping dangerously close to trees and cliffs and barren rocks. But someone kept tugging at his sleeve and calling to him, "K'leu! K'leu!" And why was his naval title being used here on top of a mountain in the Bavarian Alps?

He awoke irritably to find Hans Pohl shaking him firmly. "Wake up, K'leu, it's time."

Sitting up abruptly Werner saw Inga Brandt peering anxiously over his exec's shoulder. "What's our position?" he asked, shaking the sleep from his mind and already sensing that the boat was traveling on the surface and making about ten knots through a calm sea as the starboard diesel pounded rhythmically.

"We've just crossed the Arctic Circle, K'leu. You said to awaken you. Cape Dyer is eighty miles off the port beam. The gale passed us several miles to eastward. Wind's now out of the west at twenty knots; visibility ten miles; temperature thirty-six degrees Fahrenheit."

"Anything on radar?" Werner stepped into the passageway and climbed through the forward hatch into the control room as Hans and Inga followed.

"Nothing but ice, K'leu. More and more ice."

It had been a full forty-eight hours since they had first entered the strait. They were now some twenty-seven hundred miles from Bergen. Werner asked Hans, "How much oil in the bunkers?"

"Seventy-three tons, K'leu. And a full charge on both batteries."

"How long have we been surfaced?" He glanced over the dials and gauges, then stepped to the chart table to study the plot.

"Almost eight hours this time. It's 0840 hours. Jürgen has the watch."

Werner looked closely at his exec. "Any more sabotage?"

"No, K'leu."

Werner had worried himself to sleep trying to figure out who might have smashed the radio, who among the many aboard was most likely. He had finally settled on the navigator, Karl Axmann, simply because he had been the only one to express any open reluctance to attempt the passage. But he couldn't be sure. He had told Hans and the chief both to keep an eye on him. He would have had a twenty-four-hour guard posted on the inverted fathometer, except that its parts were in the control room and on the bridge, both places where no one was ever alone.

Crossing the control room, he glanced at the chronometer on the forward bulkhead. They had to keep adjusting it as they moved westward. With the nearly constant daylight, their sense of time was becoming meaningless. He noticed that Karl Axmann and one of the electrical artificers were at the gyro, working on some latitude adjustment, and he noted with satisfaction that they were being carefully supervised in their work by Horst Wolff.

Stifling a yawn, he accepted a mug of steaming coffee from a sailor who was passing them around, then took one sip and looked up, startled. "Ach, but this is real coffee!" He tried to think when was the last time he had a cup of anything but the inferior coffee substitute he had been drinking.

Hans Pohl was grinning over his own mug. "Compliments of our General Henke," he said. "You can have real chocolate too, if you like. Two cases of each in the stores. And American cigarettes. The Herr General has been ingratiating himself by passing them out among the crew."

Werner frowned, but continued sipping the hot aromatic brew. "Oddly generous of our general, don't you think, Hans?" But he looked at Inga Brandt and winked. "You're having chocolate?"

She nodded.

"Then I guess we'll accept the general's largess with gratitude."

Moving back to the chart table, where Karl had dutifully plotted their projected course clear up into Baffin Bay, he looked over at Inga again and smiled as he tapped the chart. "Here's where we are, Frau Brandt. Shall we go up top and take a look?"

Finishing their drinks, they climbed the tower ladder and emerged onto the open, windswept bridge under an almost clear sky. Brilliant sunshine glanced off an emerald sea and shone on the ice that sparkled everywhere around them, from the great white bergs to the bluish iron-hard growlers the size of small whales, bobbing, grumbling and grunting in the swells.

Werner glanced at the gyro repeater to confirm their course, and then at Jürgen Heuser, the second engineer, who was standing at the periscope standard surrounded by the four lookouts. He called down frequent course changes to the helmsman to maneuver the boat among the thickening floes.

"Guten Morgen, K'leu," Jürgen greeted him. "Is our young Karl still sulking because we're not taking the direct route to Argentina?" Jürgen's black eyepatch covered an eye lost to flying shrapnel. That, combined with his old dueling scar which was not quite hidden by his full black beard, gave his features a fiercely piratical leer.

"He's down below adjusting the compass."

"Be careful he doesn't adjust it all the way around and take us south instead of north."

They were all inhaling deeply of the sharp, clean arctic air when General Henke's voice called up for permission to mount the bridge. Werner smiled at Inga. "He's learning." He called down for Henke to come ahead.

Moments later the general heaved himself out of the hatch and joined them on the railed platform of the wintergarten. Hunching over with his back to the wind he managed to get fire from his gold lighter to the tip of his cigarette, then held it in its glittering holder and surveyed the world around them like an Eastern potentate. "The solid pack ice," he asked at last, "how far now?" He was looking at Inga.

"It's hard to tell, Herr General. The ice is getting steadily heavier. This around us is from newly-formed bergs—this year's ice. But from the looks of those," she pointed, "that's drift ice, probably calved off the glaciers on Greenland's west coast and drifting south on the Labrador Current. It takes them several years to reach Labrador. I'd guess the solid pack itself is maybe twenty or thirty miles ahead yet."

"Well, Inga," Werner said, "pick one of those big ones. We're going to have to go under it and test the inverted fathometer."

She looked around and finally pointed. "That one's roughly ten meters high, Kapitän. So with maybe seven-eighths of it under water, you'll have to go deeper than seventy meters to clear it."

"Is it wise to take unnecessary risks, Kapitän?" Henke suggested solicitously. "We'll have plenty of ice over us soon enough."

"We'd better find out if the damn thing works, Herr General," Werner answered, "while there's still time to correct it if it doesn't. Anyway, we're not taking a vote on it. We're testing the instrument. So please put out your cigarette and go below now."

While Henke retreated peevishly down the hatch, Werner ordered Jürgen to circle around the berg to be sure there was clearance on the far side. The giant berg glittered brilliantly on the side toward the sun, but on the shadowed faces and in the cracks and crevices it was a pale diamond-blue.

"Old ice," Inga commented. "An accumulation of years, and iron-hard. Give it plenty of clearance, Kapitän, especially on the windward side. There's usually a large projection just beneath the water. And they sometimes turn over unexpectedly."

Werner nodded, cupping a gloved hand over the voicepipe, "Stop the engine, Chief. Couple up both motors. Ahead dead slow. And get Fritz Oder on the inverted fathometer." Oberbootsmann Oder had proved to be his best technician. "Steersmann, come to bearing two-seven-five." He looked at Jürgen. "Clear the bridge,

Obersteuermann. Prepare to dive."

As the second engineer and the four lookouts scrambled below, Werner looked at Inga Brandt. "Our moment of truth, as they say." He helped her down the open hatch and cast one last glance at the berg before going down himself and securing the cover over their heads. "Take her down, Chief," he ordered as he stepped off the ladder into the control room. "Nice and easy."

The electric motors hummed as Horst Wolff signaled the planesmen and the men at the hydraulic manifold. The levers snapped against their stops. Water gurgled into the tanks and the lights on the flooding table flickered green as the boat slowly angled down by the bow. Werner, bracing himself at the chart table, glanced from the falling needle on the depth gauge to Fritz Oder at the inverted fathometer. "Give me a continuous audible readout, Oberbootsmann."

"Jawohl, K'leu. We're six meters deep now. No contact with the ice yet."

Werner looked at the chart. There was plenty of water under them. The bottom of Davis Strait here was some nine hundred fathoms below. The boat continued its dive.

"Ice contact, sir," Oder reported methodically. "Eighteen meters above us."

Werner glanced over at Henke who was standing by the port motor switchboard, and he noticed that the general's head, along with everyone else's in the control room, had unconsciously tilted upwards, as if they could see the heavy solid mass hanging over them instead of the maze of painted pipes sparkling with condensation.

"Sixteen meters to the overhead ice, sir." Oder's voice seemed extraordinarily loud in the suddenly silent control room. "Fourteen meters."

"More angle on the bow, Chief," Werner ordered. "Sharpen the descent."

"Twelve meters," Oder droned. "Fourteen. Sixteen."

Werner glanced at the needle of the depth gauge, which was flickering past sixty meters as they continued diving.

"Sixteen meters to the ice," Oder reported. "Sixteen. Sixteen. Fourteen. Twelve . . ."

"Verdammte! Flood another fifty liters, Chief," Werner ordered, and more water gurgled into the forward tanks as the angle on the bow steepened.

"Ten meters to the ice, sir. Ten. Ten . . ."

The depth gauge needle flickered past eighty meters as the boat's steel hull began to groan with the steadily increasing pressure. "Twelve meters to ice, sir. Ten meters. Ten. Sixteen meters to the ice, sir. Twenty meters!"

"Level off at ninety meters, Chief," Werner ordered, and noticed absently that Henke's mouth was gaping open like a fish out of water.

"Twenty meters. Twenty-five. Thirty . . ." Oder droned on in his professional monotone, and they could all feel the tension in the control room easing. "Forty meters to the ice, sir. Sixty. Seventy. Eighty. We're clear, sir! Echo's coming back from open water. Ninety meters!"

"Take her up slow, Chief," Werner ordered, starting up the tower ladder. "Periscope depth and hold her."

Climbing into the periscope seat in the tower, Werner worked the foot pedals and pressed his eyes to the rubber cup as he brought down the handles and adjusted the lense. Swinging the scope clear around, he brought it to bear on the berg which was behind them now. "Surface, Chief," he ordered, and as air shrieked into the tanks and the U-boat heaved herself back up onto the surface, he climbed on up to the bridge.

With a quick glance around he called down the voicepipe, "Send up the lookouts and secure from diving stations, Chief. Start the port diesel and compressors and bring the batteries back to full charge. Hans, get us back on course for Baffin Bay."

Hans joined him on the bridge as he continued their maneuver through the thickening ice flows. "It works, K'leu," the exec said, grinning. "Now the real voyage can begin."

"Yes," Werner nodded thoughtfully. "It works. Let's hope it continues to work when we're under the pack itself and probing for an open lead."

Three hours later, still surfaced and maneuvering carefully on the port diesel through the narrowing corridors of water and increasing solidity of ice, they came within sight of the polar pack itself.

"Iceblink bearing three-three-zero, K'leu," a lookout reported, and Werner ordered the engine stopped. As the awesome white silence closed around them like a shroud, he and Hans and the lookouts all swept their binoculars across the northwest horizon where there was no longer any sign of open water, only a vast and endless expanse of tumbled ice, and a distant yellowish glow.

Overhead the sun too was a pale glow in a heavy overcast as Karl Axmann came up and took another sighting with his sextant. He looked genuinely dismayed at the display of solid ice before them. When he studied his tables and reported their position his voice actually trembled.

Werner had brought up the submarine's log, and he made the entry: 22 May, 1210; have met the ice pack at sixty-seven degrees north. Light westerly breeze; patches

81

of fog; temperature thirty-one degrees F.; visibility five miles.

Hans, lowering his glasses, looked at Werner and remarked soberly, "The Arctic is a lonely place, K'leu."

Werner Reutemann did not answer him. He was caught up himself in the magnitude of what they were actually attempting. Maybe for the first time, here on the open bridge at the rim of the polar pack, he finally realized the enormity of the challenge he had accepted so complacently, even arrogantly. His tiny U-boat had always seemed insignificant enough to humble him in the wide empty ocean that was the North Atlantic. But here, amid the vast and timeless expanse of arctic wastes, it seemed almost nonexistent. Almost, he remembered from somewhere, "like a mote in the eye of God."

He looked around as Inga and General Henke requested permission to come up, and nodded. Watching them after they emerged from the hatch, he noticed that even Inga looked a little awed and uncertain as she gazed northwestward. As for Henke, his sudden apprehension and concern were immediately apparent.

"You might tell the Führer this will be his last chance for some fresh air before we duck under the pack, Herr General," he said, smiling. "Maybe forever."

Henke glared at him. "I have already asked him, Kapitän. He chooses to remain below. He says to proceed."

Werner shrugged. As several growlers bobbled and snarled dangerously close and heavy chunks of loose drift ice began crashing jarringly against the rounded saddle tanks of the boat, he gave the order to Hans. "Clear the bridge, Oberleutnant. Prepare to dive."

TEN

Oberbootsmann Fritz Oder remained at the inverted fathometer as the U-boat, operating some ten fathoms beneath the ice, crept northwestward toward Baffin Bay. They hadn't been beneath the pack an hour before Oder reported an open lead above them.

The chief engineer looked questioningly at Werner, but the captain shook his head. It was too soon. But he timed their passage under the opening. After one minute, forty-eight seconds the echo was coming back from solid ice again. It meant they would have to remain alert and react quickly, because the size of the opening would be significant and he didn't want to waste battery power circling back to look for it.

Some openings would be larger than others, of course, and for the next several hours he had a chance to run their vertical rise test drills on half a dozen. Then suddenly there were no more openings, and for the next eleven hours the inverted fathometer registered nothing but solid ice above them.

There were sounds, though, strange, unearthly sounds reported by Helmut Kranz, the hydrophone operator. He handed the earphones over to Hans who shook his head, bewildered, and passed them to Werner. The captain listened to the eerie, songlike tones and frowned, then noticed Inga reaching out, "Let me—"

He handed her the set and watched her listen and then smile as she handed them back. "Seals, Kapitän, calling to each other under the ice." Later they heard what she identified as whales. When a terrifying heaving and cracking like the breaking up of a ship was heard, which they could hear even without the hydrophones, Inga explained that it was vast fields of ice shifting and overriding and grinding together. There were plenty of sounds but no further openings in the ice, and Werner began regretting not taking advantage of the earlier ones to top off the batteries and air.

Not completely trusting the inverted fathometer yet, he had kept one man in the conning tower, seated at the sky search periscope and scanning the faintly lighted ice above them. He even took an hour of the watch himself and stared through the watery blur at the greenish translucence that roofed their prison, but to no avail.

Finally, bent over the lighted chart table in the control room between Hans Pohl and Inga Brandt, he glanced worriedly from one to the other. "We're about eighty meters beneath the pack, and with the test drills nearly fifty per cent of the batteries are exhausted. We're reaching a point of no return. Inga, could it be that the leads are only near the fringes? Could there be no open leads at all deep in the pack, at least this early in the summer?"

Inga shook her head stubbornly. "There have to be leads, Kapitän. Some small, some large, but varied and scattered throughout, because the pack is always shifting. Only in midwinter is it absolutely solid; and even then an occasional opening will appear."

"Then where in hell are they?" Hans wanted to know.

Thirty minutes later Adolph Schmidt, who had relieved Oder on the inverted fathometer, reported a change in the echo sounding.

"Open water?" Werner asked, glancing anxiously at Horst Wolff. "Stand by, Chief."

"No, sir, just different."

"Get Oder back in here," Werner ordered a petty officer. "Quick! Chief, dead slow ahead, ease her up."

As compressed air hissed into the tanks, Oberbootsmann Oder climbed sleepily through the stern hatch into the control room and took over from Schmidt.

"An open lead?" Werner asked again.

"No, sir. Ice. But thin ice."

"How thin, Oder?"

The technician was sweating. "A few inches, sir. I can't really tell. Less than a foot." His voice sounded worried, apologetic.

Horst was holding the boat just beneath the ice by alternately blowing and flooding the tanks as Werner climbed into the tower and manned the periscope. The greenish blur of light was unusually bright. "Ease her up, Chief!" he called down as he folded the handles and lowered the scope. "Gently."

He let himself back down the ladder into the control room as the sound of air being forced into the tanks filled the space around them and then was superceded by the crunching, cracking, clanging noise in the tower overhead as a tremor went through the boat. They could all feel the frozen roof above them give a little.

"Flood twenty liters, Chief," Werner ordered calmly.

Water gurgled in the tanks and the boat settled deeper again.

"Now again, Chief. A little harder."

Air shrieked into the tanks again. The boat rose as everyone in the control room braced and ducked reflexively, and then winced as the icebreakers on top of the tower crashed again against the ice and through it this time, the boat lurching and rolling heavily to the surface.

"The tower's through!" Hans shouted.

"Keep her blown up against the ice, Chief," Werner ordered, scrambling up the ladder and spinning the upper hatch wheel.

A whoosh of stale air rushed out around him as he climbed on through the open hatch and out on the bridge. His face was stung by a brisk arctic wind that nearly tore his breath away. Moving to the coaming he looked around. Only the tower itself had broken through the several inches of ice, but it was enough. The air intake was clear and nothing appeared to be damaged. "Start the starboard engine, Chief!" he shouted back down the hatch. "Hook up the charge! Hans, you and Inga come on up!"

As the starboard diesel coughed and roared to life, its noisy clamor was somehow savagely comforting as it broke the Arctic's pristine stillness. Then Inga emerged from the hatch, drawing the hood of her anorak over her head, and Hans climbed out behind her. The exec was grinning in triumph and relief as all three stared around them at the sunless, blue-gray arctic day.

The lead where they had broken through extended some seventy meters on three sides and a dozen meters ahead of them, and consisted of newly frozen ice only a few inches thick. But there was no open water at all; for beyond the thinly frozen lead were ice banks several feet high, and the tumbled broken brash and block of the pressure ridges beyond them.

A brutal, empty, placid world, Werner was thinking, a world of exquisite yet deathly beauty. Then Karl Axmann's voice came up the open hatch: "Kapitän! You want me to bring up the sextant and get a sighting?"

"Come up if you like, Obersteuermann," Werner called back, "but never mind your sextant. There's no sign of the sun."

Around them there was no horizon. The grayish sky and whitish ice and blowing snow spume had all melded so it was impossible to tell where one really ended and the other began. The blue-gray day gave no hint that a sun even existed, much less where in the murky heavens it might be.

While the diesel rumbled, putting a charge on the air compressors and batteries, and driving fresh, cold arctic air throughout the boat, Werner and Hans looked over the ice pack in all directions with their binoculars, until a sudden grating, grinding noise that could be heard even above the raucous sound of their own engine startled them all.

"The pack is shifting," Inga explained calmly. "It's always on the move. Leads sometimes open and close within minutes, but most are open for hours at least, sometimes days. It's entirely unpredictable."

Around them, below the tower, the sharp broken shards of their break-through lay tumbled about like shattered glass. Beneath the ice there was the darkly shadowed outline of the fore- and afterdecks. The air temperature stood at thirty degrees, but the stiff breeze increased the chill factor. Already a coating of glaze ice had formed on the exposed steel of the bridge around them. As they talked, it began to snow.

Gradually, the grinding sounds grew louder. "We could use a weather report," Hans said, "and a bearing on that base at Thule. But without the radio—"

General Henke's head suddenly appeared in the hatchway. As he bundled himself out on the bridge without permission and stared around at the pressure ridges and the blurred, unbroken horizon of ice, Werner snapped at him, "Herr General, I'll remind you to ask permission of the duty officer before coming up. Now go below. We might have to crash dive at a moment's notice."

"Such as now, Kapitän," Inga whispered urgently beside him, even as the ice began to scrape and squeal against the base of the tower. "I think we'd better dive now. This lead is closing fast."

"Clear the bridge!" Werner ordered without hesitation, and Karl Axmann started down almost on top of the already disappearing Henke. Breaking the ice over the voicepipe cover and cupping his mittened fist, Werner called down to the control room, "Diving stations, Chief!" Then he watched the top of Inga's head vanish down the hatch as Hans Pohl followed her.

With a last look around, Werner climbed after his exec and pulled the hatch shut over his head. Spinning the wheel to dog it tight, he called out, "Take her down, Chief. Flood fifty liters."

When the engine stopped again, the humming sound of the port motor was nearly drowned out by the rush of water and the grinding, clanging sounds of the ice crunching against the tower as they broke free and nosed down into the dark, cold depths once more.

"Level off at twenty meters," Werner ordered. "Get us trimmed and back on course for Baffin Bay."

"Ice is very irregular, Kapitän," Fritz Oder at the

inverted fathometer reported. "It's varying twelve to eighteen meters above us."

Werner nodded, his eyes on the dials and gauges. "Down ten more meters, Chief."

The charge, brief as it was, had nearly filled the air cylinders and brought the batteries back up to sixty per cent. He had thought of simply trying to break up into the same lead again, but with the air temperature below freezing and the heavier ice shifting around, he was afraid of damaging the boat, or worse, getting trapped on the surface by the ice and crushed. He had weighed the risks and decided to push on, reminding himself that the melt should be increasing as they moved northwestward with the advancing summer season. The stop had cost him very little of his precious fuel oil, and he had air in the boat again and hopefully enough juice to reach another lead.

But he wondered now if there would be enough leads in the right places. When he allowed himself to think about it, the awesome chance they were taking crowded in on him. His anxious gaze met Inga's. But oddly, he found only supreme confidence and hope in her calm, green eyes.

Thirty hours and two briefly open leads later they had reached seventy degrees north latitude with the batteries again badly depleted. The magnetic compass had become nearly useless, and Karl Axmann now stoically reported a slight drift even on the gyro as Werner ordered a change in course to three-two-zero. "We'll have to plot time, speed and distance more carefully than ever, Karl," he said, "until we can get another fix. How's your dead reckoning?"

"I—" He swallowed hard and seemed unable to answer.

"Snap out of it, man," Werner told him harshly. "Lay

89

out a course through Baffin Bay to Lancaster Sound, then tell me how long by your calculations before we can enter the sound."

Working with the dividers and parallel rules, Karl quickly applied his marks to the chart. "I make it another eighty or eighty-five hours, sir, at underwater cruising speed."

"My figures make it closer to ninety," Werner answered, "but we'll go by yours. And it probably will be mostly under water, or rather under ice. I don't anticipate many leads open enough or continuing in the right direction for any long-distance surface running." He looked over at Inga Brandt. "Although you did say Baffin Bay was reported almost free of ice once?"

"I wouldn't count on that happening, Kapitän," Inga told him. "It was a fluke of nature. Of course, in the Arctic, anything can happen, for or against us."

"And even with that last charge, K'leu," the chief reported, "we've only got about fifteen hours of juice."

"Well," Werner shrugged philosophically and remarked with irony, "we can always look on the bright side. At least this way we're saving diesel fuel."

No one in the control room seemed particularly amused.

ELEVEN

"Sixteen meters to the overhead ice, Herr Oberleutnant." Adolph Schmidt at the inverted fathometer reported the sudden change to Hans Pohl who had the conn. For the past eleven hours the boat had continued on Karl Axmann's dead reckoning course into Baffin Bay without any more open leads, or even any thin ice they could break through.

Four hours ago Hans and Inga together had finally persuaded Werner to put his head down again, promising that he would be called immediately should any significant change occur. Now the air was foul again, and the batteries down to twenty per cent. Even Inga was showing signs of worry. But Hans had let Werner sleep.

"Fourteen meters to the ice," Schmidt reported. "Twelve meters."

Oberleutnant Hans Pohl stepped to the intercom. "Kapitän to the control room."

"Ten meters." A trace of anxiety had crept into Schmidt's voice.

With a glance at the depth gauge, Hans gave another order to Jürgen Heuser. "Down another twenty meters, Obersteuermann."

As the boat flooded down and the bow angle steepened,

the captain climbed red-eyed through the forward hatch, glancing immediately at the dials and gauges. Leutnant Horst Wolff was right behind him to take over from his second as Hans reported, "Ten meters to the ice, K'leu, and closing, even though we're diving. And we're down to a twenty per cent charge. I've shut off most of the auxiliary equipment and put the planes and steering gear on manual control."

"Eight meters to the overhead ice, sir," Schmidt reported. "Seven meters. Six."

"Take her deep, Chief," Werner ordered as he and Horst took over. "More angle on the bow." He watched the angle indicator needle move to thirty degrees as the depth gauge flickered past the hundred meter mark. "Take her to one-fifty, Chief."

Horst signaled for more water in the forward tanks and full dive on both the bow and stern planes as the boat began to groan in protest. Schmidt reported, "Four meters, sir. Three. Two meters to the ice, sir!"

"Jesus and Mary," Werner breathed. "What? Down to two hundred meters, Chief!"

The boat was angling so steeply now that they all had to brace themselves by hanging onto a pipe or valve or wheel. At that moment Wilhelm Henke climbed clumsily through the forward hatch. "Why are we diving so deep, Reutemann? The Führer wants to know our position immediately, and he needs more oxygen in the forward torpedo room."

"Not now, Herr General," Werner said and turned to Horst while the moaning, creaking sounds increased in volume, echoing through the compartments as the unaccustomed pressure exerted itself on the U-boat's steel plates.

"Five meters to the overhead ice, sir. Five. Five."

With the continued distressing sounds of the boat's aging plates, Henke's expression became frozen in fear.

"Trim and hold her at two hundred, Chief," Werner ordered. As the deck leveled under them, the boat continued to protest the extreme depth.

"Four meters to ice, sir," Schmidt reported grimly. "Four. Four. Three meters."

Werner swore again under his breath and met the chief's anxious gaze. "Down another ten meters, Horst," he ordered quietly.

The bow dipped and the boat groaned hideously. Then a sudden sharp whistling sound echoed through the gangway, drowning out the other sounds as the intercom crackled: "High pressure lead leaking, sir," the motor room reported.

"Mein Gott! Stop!" Henke suddenly shrieked hysterically and lunged at Werner. "Stop! You've got to—"

Werner backhanded the general across the face even as Hans grabbed him and forced him back against the tower ladder.

"Hold him there," Werner ordered.

"Relax, Herr General," Hans's voice was tight and vicious as his forearm braced Henke's neck against the steel rungs. "You're upsetting the Kapitän's concentration. We might have to go even deeper."

"Please," the general breathed hoarsely. "Gott en Himmel."

"Four meters to the ice," Schmidt reported in a shocked, dead monotone. "Four. Four."

With a worried glance at Horst, Werner stepped to the intercom: "Frau Brandt to the control room!"

They waited amid the whistling, groaning, dripping

sounds around them that accompanied the streams of water from ruptured overhead lines as the U-boat crept along at barely two knots, almost seven hundred feet deep and still in danger of colliding with the ice. Then Inga climbed through the forward hatch and the captain looked at her incredulously. "What are we trying to get under? Can the pack ice actually be this thick? We're over two hundred meters deep!"

"Change course, Kapitän," the woman said calmly. "This particular ice might extend a thousand feet down. You've got to get around it."

Without hesitation, almost instinctively, Werner ordered a course change. "Port ten degrees!" he called to the helmsman.

"Four meters to the ice, Kapitän," Schmidt droned. "Four meters. Three."

"Down another ten, Chief."

Horst Wolff signaled the technicians. As the boat went down the sounds increased in volume. The intercom crackled again: "Engine room, propeller packing leaking, Kapitän."

"Can you fix it?" Werner asked, his eyes still on the depth gauge needle.

"Not at this depth, K'leu, too much pressure."

"You'll kill us all!" Henke hissed at Werner. "We'll be crushed!"

"Shut up, Herr General," growled Hans, who was still holding Henke against the ladder, and he increased the pressure of his forearm.

"Down another ten, Chief," Werner ordered.

As the needle on the depth gauge flickered at two hundred thirty meters, the stressful sounds the boat was making grew ominous. Around them the icy water spurted from a dozen pressure leaks. Water was already rising above the bilges in spite of the steady thump of the pumps.

"Four meters to the ice. Four meters. Five. Eight meters, Kapitän! Twelve. Eighteen."

"Slow rise, Chief," Werner ordered, beginning to breath a little easier at last.

Air hissed into the tanks. "Twenty meters to the ice, Kapitän. Thirty."

Gradually, as the boat crept slowly upwards and the pressure decreased, the insidious moaning ceased and the leaks slowed to a trickle.

"Engine room, Kapitän," the intercom reported. "Leak in the propeller packing stopped."

Hans had released Henke, who was rubbing vigorously at a sore neck but seemed otherwise subdued. Then for the first time Werner noticed his navigator standing braced beside the chart table, his knuckles white, his face chalky, his eyes still wide with sheer terror. The captain gave him a quick smile. "Cheer up, Karl, we made it."

The young navigator swallowed twice, yet couldn't seem to respond. But at least the terrible fear retreated from his eyes, and his grip on the chart table relaxed. Werner knew now he had made a serious mistake in accepting him simply because of his navigation record and ignoring his lack of battle experience. He would never have made a U-boat man, and the farther they penetrated into the Arctic, the more his depression seemed to deepen.

The rest of the crew seemed resigned, or at least indifferent. He felt Hans and maybe Horst were the only true optimists aboard, they and Inga Brandt. The three of them seemed to have more faith in Werner than he had in himself.

"Eighty meters to the overhead ice, Kapitän," Schmidt reported. The depth gauge stood at one hundred meters again, and Werner looked at Inga. "The ice is still some twenty meters thick. What in hell are we passing under or around?"

"A rafted curtain of ice, Kapitän, where two massive floes come together and override. We could meet some that extend even deeper."

"Well, you were right about maneuvering around it instead of diving under it. I'll have to remember that."

"Except that won't always work either, Kapitän. Sometimes they're several miles wide."

Werner smiled wistfully. "Don't be so encouraging, Frau Brandt. I'm liable to appoint you morale officer."

Thirty minutes later it was no longer a joking matter, even for Werner. They were running twenty meters under the ice, with only some three hours left on the batteries and most of the crew developing a dry, hacking cough from the stale air that was now laden with carbon dioxide from their own breaths.

Ordering a zigzag course now, in a desperate search for an open lead or even a patch of thin ice, Werner had Oder relieve Schmidt on the inverted fathometer. He then had the air freshened a little from the reserve oxygen tanks while the petty officers distributed potash cartridges to crew and passengers alike.

Henke demanded that more oxygen be pumped into the forward torpedo room for the Führer and Eva, but Werner merely had Chief Petty Officer Bruno Haupmann show him how to adjust the potash box around his neck and fit the rubber hose in his mouth. He gave him two more to take to Hilter's compartment.

Werner himself climbed into the conning tower where

he manned the search periscope to scan the overhead ice, more for something to keep his mind and hands busy and to get away from the watchful stares of the others than for any hope that he might spot an open lead the fathometer somehow missed.

Below them was a thousand fathoms of crushing depths. Their only hope was a break in the ice above, and Werner thanked whatever gods there might be that he had insisted on bringing at least three torpedoes. He was about to order one fired in a final and drastic attempt to break through when the area in the scope suddenly lightened perceptibly above him just as Oder in the control room below reported, "Open water, Kapitän! Ice free open water!" He nearly shouted his relief.

"Surface, Chief!" Werner shouted back. "Dead slow ahead." He watched the light intensity brighten through the scope, the water changing from gray to green to blue. Soon the scope was awash. He closed its handles and activated the periscope motor which sent it humming back into its well as the top of the tower erupted into open water.

Throwing open the hatch, Werner climbed out. While the fresh, razor-edged air burned in his lungs, he ordered the motor stopped and the port diesel started, and then the air compressors and blowers. He stepped to the coaming and gazed around at a hundred meters of open water on all sides, water covered with small bobbing pieces of pancake ice.

Best of all, the lead seemed to continue on a west by northwesterly course, extending as far as he could see. Visibility was a good ten miles. It was nearly 2100 hours, but the sun was shining through low, ragged clouds, turning the ice to a dazzling golden hue. A half-moon hung low and pale just above the horizon.

Bending over the open hatch, the rank stale air pouring up from below as a stark contrast to the raw, cold freshness around him as he called up Karl and the lookouts. He then paused a moment, listening to the comforting rumble of the diesel as it put on the charge before cupping a mittened hand over the voicepipe: "Port two degrees, Steersmann. Signal the engine room for a steady eight knots."

"Get us a fix, Obersteuermann," he ordered as the navigator pulled himself out onto the bridge behind the lookouts, sextant in hand. But Karl Axmann only stood there, staring around as if seeing the endless panorama for the first time. "Karl," Werner urged him gently, "the sightings. You've got the sun and moon both, man."

"Jawohl, K'leu," he answered woodenly. The spell apparently broken, the navigator brought the sextant to his eye and began adjusting the knobs.

"Kapitän to the control room!" Hans's voice came up the open hatch.

Werner hesitated, then shrugged off a sudden instinctive reluctance to relinquish command to his young navigator, however briefly. "Take the conn, Obersteuermann. Keep us centered in this lead as long as it continues to bear northwesterly."

"Jawohl, K'leu."

Lowering himself down the hatch and through the tower into the control room, he found Hans in a serious conversation with the chief engineer. They both gave him worried looks. "That deep dive put too much strain on her, K'leu," Hans said. "Horst thinks if we go that deep again we'll probably just keep on going."

"Do you agree with him, Hans?"

"Yes, K'leu."

"Then we'd better not have to go that deep again. We'll try to go around them." He looked at Inga who was standing beside them. "Right, Frau Brandt?"

"Our position, Kapitän," Karl's voice came down the hatch, "I make it 70-39 North, 64-10 West."

Moving to the chart table, Werner quickly plotted the figures on the chart. "That places us here," he pointed for Hans and Inga who had stepped up beside him, "some three hundred fifty miles southeast of the entrance to Lancaster Sound and the Northwest Passage." He looked around at the others. "Not bad. I must congratulate our young navigator. And it also places us about four hundred miles from the Danish-American weather station at Thule. I'd give a solid gold barnacle for a weather report."

"Hard to port!" The sudden order shouted down to the helmsman from the bridge startled them all. Werner grabbed the chart table as the helmsman put the wheel over and the boat listed sharply, slewing in the sudden turn.

"Was ist los? We're turning southwest!" Hans shouted as a second order came down.

"Couple up the starboard engine. Both ahead full!"

Even as Werner lurched toward the ladder he heard the engine telegraph and then the starboard engine firing as a second voice, distant and muffled, shouted, "Kapitän to the bridge!"

Werner banged both knees on the ladder as he climbed through the lower hatch into the tower shouting, "Hold that order. Slow ahead both!" He was uncertain what could have happened, but he dreaded the worst.

As he emerged through the upper hatch onto the bridge

he saw it was too late. The boat was headed straight for the broken ice at the southwest edge of the lead, ice now only a few meters away as the water formed around the bow and Karl Axmann, with both hands gripping the coaming, stared straight ahead.

The lookout had turned from him to the captain as Werner shouted down the voicepipe: "Reverse engines! Emergency! Both astern full!" But he knew it was in vain. The low ice bank was too close, looming nearer and nearer, seeming to rush at them even as the reversing engines churned in a maddening, vibrating torque of panic.

Turning was out of the question. Putting the helm over in either direction would only let the jagged ice rip open the saddle tanks. "Secure for a bow collision!" Werner shouted in anguish down the voicepipe, then braced himself with the lookouts against the bridge rails just before the U-boat hit.

TWELVE

With a grinding, screeching crash the U-boat struck the ice bank and kept on going. Instead of bursting asunder, the curved bow slid up onto the ice, rearing up to a thirty degree angle, seeming to poise there motionless for an eternity before the great cracking sounds of the ice breaking under the weight of the steel hull resounded in the clear arctic air. The heavy boat suddenly plunged downward, crashing through the ice into the water again, where the propellers, still churning in reverse, pulled her slowly back out into the open water of the lead.

"Stop engines!" Werner called down the voicepipe. "Damage report! Are we taking any water?"

"Negative, K'leu," the tight, strained voice of the chief engineer came back. "But I'm glad we won't have to try to open the outer doors of the bow torpedo tubes. They're probably jammed."

"K'leu!" One of the lookouts touched Werner's shoulder and pointed to where the figure of a man was running across the ice, running away from the gaping hole they had just put in the bank. "It's Obersteuermann Axmann, K'leu," the sailor explained. "He climbed down to the deck. While the bow was hung up he jumped ashore!"

"Karl!" Werner called, cupping his mittened hands to

his mouth. "Karl! Come back!" Bringing his binoculars to his eyes, he focused them on the fleeing figure. But the navigator wasn't even looking back. Slipping occasionally and falling, he'd scramble to his feet and hurry on, heading south.

"Kapitän! Are we sinking?" General Henke came struggling up through the hatch.

"No," Werner answered without taking his glasses from the fleeing navigator. "But it was close, Herr General. How are the Führer and his wife?"

"Safe, Gott sei dank. They were sleeping in their bunks. What are you looking at? What happened?"

"We've lost Karl Axmann, Herr General. That's him out there. He ran us ashore and took off on foot across the ice. He seems determined to go south."

"But," Henke sputtered, "the navigator! We've got to stop him!"

Lowering his glasses, Werner looked at the SS general. "I'll be glad to put you ashore if you care to try."

"Shall we go after him, K'leu?" one of the lookouts volunteered.

"Yes, break out a dinghy. He shouldn't run far. Mein Gott!" Karl Axmann had slipped trying to climb over a smooth, round hummock of ice. Werner had raised his glasses again just in time to see him slide spread-eagled to the bottom where he just disappeared through a dark hole in the ice.

In that one instant the Arctic had swallowed him. Weighted with his seaboots and heavy clothes, he never even reappeared. "Never mind the dinghy," Werner said, lowering the glasses. He noticed with somewhat guilty relief that Karl had left the sextant behind. It was still cradled safely on the shelf below the coaming.

"But how can we find our way without him?" Henke asked, still awed by the suddenness of the death.

Werner shook his head wearily. "I've been known to navigate myself, Herr General. And if I go mad too too, there's always Hans. So you're in safe hands, you and the Führer." He looked again at the place where Karl had disappeared, evidently a seal's breathing hole, and murmured more to himself than to anyone else, "I suppose the poor devil smashed the radio too, thinking we wouldn't go further north without weather reports."

"I smashed your radio, Kapitän," General Henke admitted stiffly, almost proudly. "At the Führer's orders."

"What? You smashed the radio?" Werner turned on him in a sudden rage. The loss of young Karl and now this news was almost too much, and his mittened hands gripped the bridge rails to keep them from going for the general's throat.

Henke shrank back a step from Werner's fierce gaze, but quickly recovered some of his blustering defiance. "After that last communique, the Führer wanted no more news of the Allied occupation of our glorious Fatherland. He found it demoralizing."

"Henke," Werner stepped forward, bringing his face close to the general's, "if you ever give or carry out any order again aboard this boat without my express permission, I'll put you and the Führer out there on the ice with Karl!" Then, turning his back on an equally enraged and flustered general, Werner gave the conn over to Jürgen who had joined them on the bridge and stormed angrily below.

In the control room he found Helmut Kranz, who doubled as medic, binding a splint on the chief's forearm. Horst winced, then grinned sheepishly through his pain.

"Clumsy of me, K'leu, but the sudden turn caught me by surprise. A simple fracture."

"Anyone else hurt?" Werner asked, glancing around but still so angry with both Henke's confession and Karl's foolish act that he ignored Inga's concerned expression as she stood anxiously by the chart table.

"No other casualties, K'leu," Hans Pohl reported. "A few bruises and scrapes, but everyone managed to grab onto something except the chief. What happened up there?"

"Obersteuermann Axmann decided to head south on foot. He ran us aground and jumped ship. Then he fell through a hole in the ice and was gone in an instant. Fortunately, when we hit, our curved bow slid out of the water onto the ice like a sled on runners and then broke through harmlessly, at least I hope harmlessly. We haven't tried out the bow dive planes yet." He looked at Horst Wolff, whose usually ruddy face was a little pale. "You want to lie down awhile, Chief?"

Horst shook his head. "I'm all right. Kranz gave me a shot. He'll set it later."

"Lie down anyway. That's an order. I'll send Jürgen down to start the port engine and resume the charge on the batteries and air." He turned to his exec. "Hans, come up top with me and get us on course for Lancaster Sound. I'm going to get another fix on our position, just to make sure." He looked again at Inga, and by now his mood had softened and he motioned her to follow them.

Out on the bridge the temperature stood at thirty-one degrees, with a stiff, chilling wind out of the east and the sun a pale white glow low in a tumbled grayish sky as Werner raised the sextant for another sighting.

The port diesel throbbed heavily, rhythmically as Hans

ordered the bow brought around. Once again they began to follow the broad, westerly-winding lead through the ice at eight knots, while Wilhelm Henke huddled morosely in his greatcoat at the farthest rail of the wintergarten, staring aft. No one paid him any more attention.

"It's close," Werner said after consulting the tables and jotting the figures in his notebook. "Looks like Karl's last official act was to give us a true position."

"But it was a narrow escape, wasn't it?" Inga asked. She was standing beside him as he put away the sextant and navigation tables.

"I thought it was our finish," Werner answered. "I was never so surprised in my life as when the bow reared up on the ice instead of smashing into it."

"The ice is tricky," Inga said. "The very hardness of it probably saved us. Had it been newer, softer ice it might have broken instead, and the sharp shards sliced into your hull, ripping it open like a can." She was staring out across the fogbound distant floes. "But I feel so sorry for young Karl. Why would he do such a thing?"

"He broke under the strain. It happens. Even a U-boat captain broke a couple of years ago. Shot himself in the tower of his boat while they were under depth charge attack." He looked at her long and seriously. "Nobody's invincible, Inga."

"Are you beginning to have doubts?" she asked him.

"I've never been without doubts about this voyage. But I'll tell you one thing, the farther we go the more I am convinced it can be done."

"If only Karl had had a little more faith," she sighed. "He must have been the one who smashed the radio."

"No," Werner answered, his voice hardening. "That was our friend Henke."

Startled, she glanced back at the general who was still standing on the railed platform, but he continued to ignore them. The rumble of the diesel effectively covered their conversation, but even so she found herself moving closer to Werner and whispering, "The general destroyed the radio? Why? Is he breaking too?"

Werner told her about Henke's action on the Führer's orders. "But we'll all be a little mad before this voyage is over," he added, and then he told her of another decision he'd made after considerable thought. Even if they made it safely through this incredible passage to Japan, he'd decided that somehow he would have to make sure their demented Führer didn't. "A Fourth Reich is something Germany and the world can well do without."

THIRTEEN

Northwestering on the surface for an unbelievable thirty-six hours, they followed the miraculously open channel that wound like a broad canal through the pack ice of Baffin Bay, and finally approached the wide mouth of Lancaster Sound.

The weather had held too. Fog came and went, but it had not been a problem. When it was thickest they probed their way through the ice with their radar, pushing through loose pancake and managing to avoid the larger bits and occasional growlers, though the latter were so low in the water they seldom showed on the radar screen and had to be sighted by a lookout stationed on the bow.

They'd been forced to submerge only twice by closing floes, and then each time they'd been able to surface and regain the westerly channel in less than an hour.

Now, approaching the sound, only wisps of fog hung like smoke over a silk smooth sea as the submarine's alternating diesels continued to pound faithfully, though incongruously loud, shattering the ghostly isolation and chill, blue-white world of high arctic spring that lay across their path. It all presented a mysterious, almost ethereal beauty as once again the Führer and his wife emerged through the forward hatch, bundled in their greatcoats and mufflers. This time they excercised by pacing back and forth along the slatted deck below the conning tower for some thirty minutes before returning below.

With the chief engineer conning the boat from the bridge, Werner and Hans huddled over the chart table in the control room, working out the plot from their latest sighting. Werner had told Henke they could navigate as well as Karl Axmann, which was true enough; but they also faced the same problems Karl had. Besides converging meridians and very few navigational aids, they had a magnetic compass that was nearly useless in these latitudes and needed careful adjustment and frequent checks. They even had a gyro that, though adjusted to its highest latitude of seventy degrees, was beginning to drift more and more the nearer they approached the magnetic pole. If they strayed into even one of the hundreds of icebound bays and inlets, Werner shook his head at the thought.

Thus far their luck had held. The batteries and air cylinders were fully charged once more. By alternating the diesels and moving at moderate speeds, thus conserving both fuel and the wear on each engine, they still had a good sixty-four tons of oil in the bunkers.

"Kapitän to the bridge!" Horst's voice came down the pipe and both Hans and Werner hurried up the ladder and through the open hatch.

The chief, his broken arm now set and slung snugly beneath the binoculars dangling at his chest, and the hood of his anorak thrown back so that his rust-red hair was ruffled by the rising wind, pointed toward the northwest with his free hand. "There's nothing to see, K'leu, with that fog bank out there, but listen."

The distant sound was muffled by the heavy fog, but it

was still distinct above the throb of their own engine, an irregular, sharp, metallic clanging. Werner's first thought as he raised his own glasses was the impossible likelihood of another ship in these waters, but he could see nothing either and Horst reported nothing but scattered ice patterns on the radar. The distant sounds continued at irregular intervals, sharp and repetitive, though they didn't seem to be getting any closer. Stepping to the voicepipe, Werner called down. "Frau Brandt to the bridge, please."

While they waited and the sounds continued, Horst tapped Werner on the shoulder and pointed ahead of them over the bows. "The noise wasn't the only reason I sent for you, K'leu. We're running out of seaway up ahead."

Forward of the U-boat the water lead was curving away sharply and irrevocably to the south. When Werner raised his glasses again and focused them, he could see what the chief meant. Not far ahead the westerly course of the lead was ending abruptly. It continued right on through the seemingly endless pack ice, but on a southerly course now which was of no further use to their progress.

Then Inga's hooded head appeared. As she climbed out on the windy bridge, it was obvious from her red and puffy eyes that she'd been sleeping.

"Sorry to awaken you, Frau Brandt," Werner told her, "but we have a mystery. You hear it?"

Inga, cocking her head and tugging back the edge of her furred hood, listened to the harsh and distant clanging, then nodded, smiling. "It's nothing to fear, Kapitän. As long as we don't get any closer. It's ice calving, great cliffs of ice breaking off a glacier as it melts and plunging into the sea. It makes that clanging sound. There must be glacier fields northwest of us. See," she pointed, "those great bergs drifting out of that fog?"

"I see," Werner said, but he felt annoyed with himself that he had not really seen. He had been so concerned with the strange sounds and then the sudden southerly bearing of the lead that he hadn't even noticed the new and bigger bergs drifting down on them out of the fog bank. "Well, we're going to have to dive anyway," he added. "As you can see ahead, we've lost our westerly path through the ice." He looked around at the approaching fog and icebergs and deteriorating weather. Overhead the sky was like thickly curdled cream that offered not even a hint of brightness to show where the sun might be. "Lookouts below," he ordered. "You too, Chief. Prepare to dive." He had the eerie feeling that they had see the last of the good weather and the good luck as he followed Inga and the others down the hatch.

Ten hours later, creeping westward at four to five knots some twenty meters beneath the ice, Werner put his finger at a point on the chart and grunted. "Dead reckoning puts us about here," he told Inga and Hans who were standing on either side of him, "fifty miles into the sound. If we don't find any more long, open leads, our current underwater speed won't put us into the Barrow Strait for another thirty-six hours." He looked up at Inga. "Anything you can tell us about the region that might help?"

Inga frowned, shaking her head. "Just more ice, Kapitän. It's nearly June now, so the melt is increasing. I wouldn't worry about the slowness of our speed. If we could go any faster we might only run into heavier ice accumulations and fewer open leads. And we've already moved out of range of those calving ice fields behind us. Actually, this way, time is working with us."

"And our fuel consumption is kept at a minimum," Hans added.

"But the more melting, the greater the movement and unpredictable size of the ice," Werner suggested, rubbing his bearded jaw. "And that means more deep-rafted ice caught in the moving pack."

"We can't have everything our own way, Kapitän," Inga noted gently if sarcastically.

But their luck continued strong, and in the following ten hours they found three open leads. Nothing like the one they had left behind in Baffin Bay, but two had been long enough to move at moderate speed amid pancake ice while topping off the batteries and air. In the longest lead they had run a good three hours on the surface at seven to nine knots before forced under by closing floes.

As the voyage continued, creeping along at twenty meters of depth, the distance to the overhead ice remained fairly constant. The inverted fathometer never varied more than a meter or two. Sixteen to eighteen meters above them was the solid white roof of the Arctic.

They had encountered no more great bergs in Lancaster Sound, or the dreaded deep-rafted ice; but they were approaching the Barrow Strait which would be much shallower water. So while they still had over two hundred fathoms under the keel, leaving plenty of room for maneuvering, Werner finally allowed himself a little more time away from the control room.

Leaving Hans with the conn, he went to the ward room and ate breakfast. The chronometer on the bulkhead read 0500 hours, but time was almost meaningless. At this latitude and time of year only a few minutes of twilight separated the days on the calendar. Between the eternal day above and night below, it was easy to become disoriented. And confronted now with the realities of a voyage that seemed suddenly endless, Werner gripped the mug of coffee the duty messman had brought him until his knuckles ached.

It had been another thirty hours since he had last slept and exhaustion claimed him. Yet he was charged with the incredible accomplishment thus far. He knew he had never really thought they could get this much behind them. Now he knew it could be done. Whether he succeeded or not, he knew it was at least possible that a submarine could feasibly transit the Northwest Passage under the ice. He tried to imagine what it would mean. It would revolutionize warfare, of course. But the possibilities for peaceful transport were there too, with big new Walther boats to carry cargo and remain submerged almost endlessly.

Sipping at the hot brew in his mug, he knew that even a few days ago he would never have felt the confidence he was experiencing now, in both the boat and the crew. Together they were actually defeating the ice. But he knew too he would have to guard against overconfidence. The chronic fear continued at the back of his mind. One slight mistake, one misdirection of judgement could still wipe out everything. They were still so goddamned vulnerable in the midst of all this ice. It was like feeling their way through an endless mine field.

He looked up as his ice expert stepped into the wardroom carrying a light meal on a tray. "May I join you, Kapitän?"

"Of course."

As she set it down and slid onto the bench across the table, she reached over and placed a warm hand on his. "Why can't you get more rest, Werner? Hans is capable."

He nodded. "I know." Watching her pick at the scrambled eggs and sausages, he knew she wasn't really hungry. She had come to be with him. "You know, don't you, Inga, that I didn't even realize those bergs back there were bigger and closer than before, the ones near the entrance to the sound where the ice was calving?"

"You can't be aware of everything."

"But that's the point, I must. I make the decisions that our success or failure depends on, that our lives depend on." He was acutely aware that she had stopped eating and had again placed a warm hand on his.

"You brought your boat and crew through the hazards of a war, Werner Reutemann, and now you're taking them through the hazards of an arctic ice pack. There's not really that much difference, is there?"

Werner smiled, and setting aside his mug he folded her hand in both of his. "You're good for my morale, Frau Brandt. You're good for this voyage. I can handle the boat, but we'd never have made it this far without you to handle the ice."

She blushed but didn't withdraw her hand. "The point is we are making it," she said. "And shouldn't we begin asking ourselves what then? Can we really start all over somewhere else? Do you know what was happening in the Führer's Reich, the slaughter of hundreds of thousands of Russian prisoners, the 'final solution' for the Jews?"

Werner's expression tightened visibly. "I heard the rumors the few times I was on leave. I dismissed them as enemy propaganda. I believe them now."

"Then can we really make new lives anywhere? Can we ever put all the confusion and uncertainty and mistakes behind us?"

Maybe, Werner thought, if we could only leave our consciences behind us too. Then the intercom crackled a noisy interruption and Hans's voice boomed with a note of controlled urgency. "Emergency! Kapitan to the control room! Fire in the port motor switchboard!"

FOURTEEN

Werner's brain went catatonic. For an instant he couldn't move, couldn't think. Fatigue and inertia gripped him like a vice. The worst had happened: a fire under the ice!

"Werner!" Inga's voice.

"Emergency! Fire! Kapitän to the control room!" The intercom crackled again.

Somewhere Werner found his senses and reacted, hurrying forward along the aisle, already smelling the strong acrid fumes of an electrical fire. Stepping through the hatchway into the smoke-filled control room, he pressed a handkerchief to his face and saw the sparks leaping from the switchboard as technicians fought the blaze with fire extinguishers. He realized Hans at least had it under control.

But the damned smoke! They'd suffocate. Blindly he called to Hans, "The stern torp, Exec! Get to the attack table! Make sure the settings are close enough to reach the hole in time, but far enough not to blow us up along with the ice! We've got to get on the surface and exhaust this smoke!" He began choking and coughing along with the rest of them as he watched Hans's seaboots disappear up the tower ladder. He then felt his way to the intercom. "Flood the stern tube. Prepare for firing!"

Hans, coughing, called down from the tower, "Torp set, K'leu! Range three hundred. Ready, ready. Flood forward, Chief!"

The boat tilted down by the bow and the intercom crackled with the voice of a torpedo mixer, "Stern tube ready!" Werner was grateful he'd at least had the foresight to load with old contact torpedoes instead of magnetic or acoustical ones.

"All ready, K'leu!"

"Shoot, Exec!" Werner shouted and succumbed to a spasm of coughing as he bent low to let his burning lungs escape at least the heavier layer of smoke and fumes. Everyone was on the deck of the control room now, rags or handkerchiefs pressed to their faces, as they strained to stay under the now dense smoke. Werner felt the lurch of the boat as the torpedo left the stern tube and heard the gurgle of water as Horst compensated for the sudden weight loss to hold the boat's trim.

The captain was counting the seconds. There was no time to load for a second desperate shot if the first was no good. He was considering blowing all tanks and attempting to crash upwards through the ice when he heard a muffled explosion and felt the heavy concussion against the boat's steel plates. Immediately Werner ordered hard right rudder. "Zero-nine-zero degrees, Steersmann. Bring us around to that opening, if there is an opening." Then he ordered more oxygen released from the cylinders as they all tried unsuccessfully to hold their breaths. More seconds ticked by. Fritz Oder on the inverted fathometer chokingly called out the distance to the overhead ice: "Four meters. Four. Three. Open water! We're under open water, K'leu!"

"Surface!" Werner ordered. "Blow all tanks! Hard rise

on both planes! Get us up fast, Chief! And stop motors."

Air shrieked into the tanks. As Werner climbed the ladder into the smoke-filled tower he saw Hans's dark shape already above him, waiting just under the upper hatch and gasping for breath until they felt the U-boat heave herself onto the surface. The exec spun the wheel and pushed open the lid.

Smoke rushed with the stale air up the tower and poured out on the bridge around them as they caught themselves at the edge of the coaming and hung there, retching. Then Werner called down, "Start the compressors, Chief! Ventilate the boat! Start the port diesel and hook up the charge!"

Only then did he take time to look around at the ragged hole they had made by blasting through nearly three feet of solid ice. They were floating amidst the brash and block as the port diesel kicked over with a belch of smoke. All around them the dim horizon of ice and sky were melded into one, and above them the low thick overcast was like a dirty gray blanket thrown across the top of the world.

With the diesel rumbling, putting on the charge, and the compressors and blowers filling the air cylinders and forcing fresh cold air throughout the boat, Werner had the forward hatch thrown open and let most of the crew begin filing out along the railed foredeck.

More men came up through the bridge hatch and climbed down the ladder to the afterdeck, retching and clearing their lungs. And though there was no sign of Hitler or his wife, General Henke was soon shouldering his way toward Werner and Hans and Inga who stood waiting in the wintergarten abaft the bridge where the railing was already hung with icicles, like glittering ornaments on a tree.

"We've got to turn back!" the SS general blustered, pulling up the collar of his greatcoat as he glared around them at their icebound hell. "The Führer's orders! He's had enough of this incompetence!"

Werner turned an amused glance towards Hans who was calmly lighting two cigarettes and offering one to Inga. He looked back at Henke. "How are the Führer and his lady, Herr General? Not getting too stuffy in the forward torpedo room, I hope?"

"Damn you, Reutemann!" Henke's murderous look included the smiling exec. "You too, Pohl! The Führer's had enough. It's obvious now we chose the wrong means of escape or the wrong captain to lead it. Turn back now. Before we're all killed."

"That's not possible, Herr General," Werner answered quietly. "We're more than half way now and have reached the point of no return. The fuel to turn back no longer exists. We can only go forward and hope." This wasn't altogether true. They had enough fuel to at least get back to the North Atlantic shipping lanes where they could surrender, but Werner wasn't about to turn back as long as he could find openings in the ice.

"But the Führer orders," Henke started, but stopped in midsentence.

Werner's gaze had hardened, his humor suddenly gone along with his patience. "The Führer's orders cannot change the facts, Herr General. Not here any more than in his Berlin bunker, where I heard he was maneuvering phantom divisions in imaginary counterattacks against the Allied advances just hours before he chose to escape."

Wilhelm Henke drew himself up in a livid rage. He said nothing, but a vein in his temple pulsed as he slipped a hand inside his coat and in one swift motion had the barrel of a Walther pistol shoved against Werner's flat, hard belly.

Inga cried out, and Hans started forward but was restrained by the captain's arm. "Let him be, Oberleutnant. He's brutal and crude—even a bit inhuman—but he's not stupid. Are you, Herr General? You know if you shoot me, or even Hans, the crew would show you no mercy. You do know that, don't you, Henke?"

Fear flickered now behind the outrage in the general's eyes. Slowly, he returned the pistol to its holster inside his coat and quickly changed his tactics. "Look here, Reutemann," he offered reasonably, "the Führer is our only hope of a glorious Fourth Reich. Get us back safely, somewhere, and your rewards will be boundless." Then his eyes narrowed threateningly again under bushy brows. "Refuse and a court-martial awaits you wherever we land. We have influence everywhere, Kapitän."

"But do you have any influence here, Herr General?" Again Werner smiled in the SS general's teeth. "Here on this boat where it counts? Look around you, at the crew. These are loyal German seamen, true. But loyal to Germany, to the Kriegsmarine, and to me. You see, I'm afraid the Führer no longer gives the orders, Herr General. Certainly not out here. Because the war is over. Our thousand-year Reich lasted only twelve years; so ask yourself if these loyal German sailors are still loyal enough to Herr Hitler to really start a Fourth Reich. Ask yourself if you can chance their loyalty, General, then either shoot me or go back down and tell the Führer that we really have no choice but to proceed, because we don't. And who knows, General, with continued patience and skill and a great deal of just plain good luck, we might still make it."

General Henke's eyes spoke volumes as he glared at all of them, but his recognition of who had the advantage and his fear of the alternatives were there too. "Verräter!" he muttered viciously. "Goddamned traitors, all of you!" His glare turned to include the seamen on the bridge and down on the deck beyond. "You're all traitors!" he shouted. With that he turned again, shouldering his way across the crowded bridge and arrogantly lowering his big frame back down the hatch.

When Henke had disappeared below, Hans Pohl looked seriously at Werner and shook his head. "He might have killed you, K'leu. He's as crazy as the Führer."

"If he does, my friend, then it'll be up to you and Inga to kill him and then get the boat through."

"Don't talk like that, Werner!" Inga tossed away her cigarette and moved to his side. "We will make it—all of us. But don't antagonize that beast. Hitler's finished anyway. You're right. Germans will never follow him again, or anyone like him. Not most of them anyway."

Werner smiled at her wearily. "I only wish I could be as sure of that as you are. But I wasn't joking when I said it will take a great deal of good luck to get us through. Hans knows," he glanced at his exec, "that fire and another few minutes—"

But Inga Brandt was stubborn. "We'll make it," she whispered tightly, taking his arm. "We'll beat the Führer and Henke both. And we'll beat the ice!"

The sudden stoppage of the muttering diesel and the deafening descent of the white arctic silence around them interrupted their conversation abruptly and made everyone look around anxiously. Werner exchanged glances with Hans. It was too early for the batteries to be up to full charge, or the air. Then the starboard engine coughed and came roaring to life, but minutes passed and both Werner and Hans were still wondering about the sudden change when Horst Wolff pulled himself awkwardly out on the bridge, his broken arm still held firmly against his chest in the dirty oil-streaked sling.

The chief engineer glanced around until he spotted Werner, then came striding purposefully back into the wintergarten.

"What's wrong, Chief?" Warner asked, frowning.

"Bearings froze up on the port diesel. I'm continuing the charge on the starboard engine." He had pulled out a pack of cigarettes, and as he shook one free Hans cupped a light for him. "Danke. The electrical artificers are repairing the port motor switchboard, K'leu, but if we have to depend on only one engine for recharging—" He inhaled deeply and shook his head, not finishing the thought.

"What about spare bearings?" Werner asked irritably, wondering why the engineer was bothering him with this.

Horst Wolff met his captain's gaze. "There aren't any, K'leu. My fault. I stocked every spare part aboard myself, and the spare bearings are checked off on the manifest. But they're just not there."

"Not there?" Werner swore softly, bitterly. By alternating the two diesels, they always had a spare. Now, if the starboard engine failed too, they wouldn't be able to charge the batteries, and the electric motors would soon be useless as well. He stared hard at his chief engineer. "We need that engine, Horst."

FIFTEEN

A thick fog bank that had been gathering broke up and blew away, but the temperature continued to drop along with the barometric pressure. Visibility remained poor, and a chilling wind stood out of the north, driving most of the crew back down below. Only a few still lounging for a last smoke stood along the railing of the fore- and afterdecks.

Inga too had gone below, out of the deepening cold, and only Hans and Werner and a brooding chief engineer remained on the open bridge, along with the lookouts. The starboard engine continued to throb, building the charge, but the opening they had blasted in the ice was gradually closing. Already there was no longer any open water around them, only a frozen slush that seemed to be hardening by the minute.

Werner, moving to the voicepipe, called down to the second engineer. "Jürgen, how much of a charge have we got?"

"Almost seventy per cent, K'leu!"

Werner looked around them at the lowering sky and the solidifying ice and glanced at Hans. "Seventy per cent will have to do," he decided. "Get the rest of the crew below, Exec. We're going under."

Turning back would now have to be considered, though it would be almost as dangerous as forging ahead. While Hans stepped to the coaming and called down the order to clear the decks and secure the forward hatch, the still brooding chief engineer stared for a long moment at his cigarette butt and then suddenly grinned broadly as he flicked it over the side and turned to Werner. "K'leu, I have an idea. But I'll need the foil from the crews' cigarette packages."

"The what?"

"The tinfoil around their cigarette packs. Maybe their chocolate bars too." His ruddy face was glowing now with inspiration and relief. "I'm going to make bearings for the goddamned port engine."

Ten minutes later they submerged in a howling blizzard, slipping back into the dark, cold, silent depths, accompanied only by the constant humming sound of the starboard electric motor. With the inverted fathometer once more seeking out the distance to the overhead ice, and using their last celestial fix along with dead reckoning, they resumed their westerly probe and entered the Barrow Strait.

Horst Wolff, busy in the engine room with the foil they had hurriedly gathered from the crew, was happy as a maid in her kitchen. Werner Reutemann, bent over the lighted chart table with Hans in the control room, made one more neatly lettered entry in the U-boat's log, and once again counted his blessings. With the port motor switchboard repaired, and the port diesel well on the way, there was once more the bitter-sweet hope of success for his fantastic mission.

Inga Brandt thought so too. In fact she had never given up hope. Even with the outbreak of fire in the control room, her faith in Werner's ability to extricate them from every difficulty held supremely firm. The threat of fire had certainly proved real enough, but it was mitigated somewhat by the knowledge they could blast their way to the surface if they had to—if they didn't run out of torpedoes, and if neither of the two remaining ones were duds, that is.

Seated now at the small desk in Werner's compartment, she knew that she was in love with the man. Had known it from the beginning, she supposed, since she had first seen him standing there with the flotilla commandant in Bergen.

She shuddered involuntarily, still cold, and realized that the cold had become a constant element now, even inside the boat. In spite of the heavy clothing and the comforting, whirring sound of the heaters, there was this ever-present penetration of frigid arctic chill and dampness permeating the entire boat. She found herself shivering uncontrollably and staring apprehensively at the condensation on an unpaneled portion of the bulkhead. Faced with a sudden and sickening premonition of doom, she forced it out of her thoughts, replacing it with daydreams, fantasizing about herself and Werner. They'd make it to Japan, to Argentina, to a new life, a fresh start, together.

In the corridor outside, Werner paused at the closed curtain of his compartment, not realizing he had passed right by the bunk he had been sharing with Hans in the wardroom. So tired now, he could hardly keep his eyes open, he had once more turned over the conn to Hans. From force of habit and perhaps of extreme fatigue he had inadvertently come to his own quarters, which he hadn't used since this voyage began.

He started to turn back when he realized where he was, then paused, thinking he might at least look in on Inga as long as he was here. He knocked hesitantly on the edge of the bulkhead.

"Who's there?"

"Werner. Is everything all right?"

A moment passed before the curtain was drawn aside and she was standing there looking up at him. "Yes, I'm fine. But you look terrible. Come in."

"Just for a moment." He let her lead him inside where she closed and clipped the curtain shut behind him. "I'm going to try and get some sleep," he said. "I've told Hans to wake me at the next open lead."

She turned to him. "You're just not getting enough rest, Werner." Gently, she forced him into the chair at his desk. "Can't Hans raise the boat at the next lead and put on the charge?"

"It's my responsibility, Inga."

"I know, I know," she answered wearily, a strange bitterness edging into her voice. "We Germans all had our responsibilities throughout the war, and we carried them out with our typical German efficiency."

So she felt it too, Werner thought, the guilt. For that's what it was, sheer guilt. He was often haunted by the Allied seamen he had put on the bottom, and ironically even by his own comrades-in-arms, his fellow U-boat men, most of whom were on the bottom now too. It made him feel guilty for having survived. What was he doing here, escaping through this frigid nightmare to nowhere? Somehow it wasn't right, his even being alive. Somehow it disturbed the rest of the honorably dead sailors on both sides, sailors smothered in oil, burned and drowned and blown to bits. It disturbed his rest.

But he was surprised that she could feel guilt. Could it be they would all feel the crushing weight of their collective responsibility for having followed the leadership of a madman who even now rode the bows of his U-boat?

"Werner," she murmured, standing very close. "I'm so cold. Warm me. Now."

He stood up, holding her, their bodies melding as she tilted her head back and her eyes moistened. "I'm in love with you, Werner Reutemann," she said simply.

"Inga," he whispered, "Inga."

"Werner?" she murmured against his shoulder. "Will we ever see spring again? Will we ever walk green fields and float serenely under sail in a warm summer breeze? Will we ever do these things, Werner, together?"

He started to tell her the truth, that he didn't know, he couldn't be sure, but he caught himself. The truth would have broken the spell, and already they were no longer in the cold cramped quarters of a dank, foul-smelling U-boat groping blindly under the ice. Already they were soaring up and away. "Ja, Liebchen," he murmured into her hair. "Ja, ja, we will do all those things and more together. I promise."

With the curtain clipped shut behind them, they lay down together fully clothed on the narrow bunk. And they held each other close. They touched. They kissed. They soothed and comforted and warmed each other. Damn the boat and the Führer and the ice, thought Werner. Damn everything! Just for a little while he let love and fatigue and oblivion sweep joyously over them both.

It was a joy he hadn't known in years. And because he knew it couldn't be his for long he wanted desperately to savor it, to prolong it, to steal it selfishly and make it his own, if only for a little while. And for a little while he did. For the first time in six years he let his iron resolve slowly relax and his steel self-discipline melt away. He allowed himself this one truly human moment, a moment that stretched away into a blissful, joyful eternity.

SIXTEEN

General Wilhelm Henke, climbing cold and stiff from his bunk in the officers' wardroom, stepped out into the passageway and caught himself as the U-boat lurched in making a course correction. We must be on the surface again, he thought miserably, following another opening through the goddamned ice. That would account for the fresh air pouring from the blowers too, but even this knowledge failed to revive his spirits, and digging out his chased silver flask he sipped at the fine Napoleon brandy that had never failed to warm him before.

Now, even staying half drunk most of the time didn't warm him. "Verflucht!" he cursed solemnly, leaning heavily against a bulkhead and taking another tug at the flask. He had been awakened from a deep sleep by a sailor who had said the Führer wanted to go up on deck. He had told the fool to let him go wherever he damn well pleased, that he was the Führer. Why had the idiot bothered him? He was tired of playing wet nurse to Hitler. Now he was too cold to get back to sleep and in a worse mood than ever.

He cursed as the boat lurched again and brought him up short outside Inga's quarters where the green curtain was tightly closed as if in deliberate defiance.

Henke stood there a moment, staring at the offending curtain, taking it as a personal affront. Cold and miserable and frightened, and angry with himself for being frightened, he was also sick of this crowded, dirty, stinking boat and everyone aboard it, especially that Werner Reutemann and his ice expert! But even Hitler too, and his slut Eva. "Scheissdreck!" he swore again. He was finally drunk enough to admit it. It was all a great madness. And it wasn't fair. He deserved better than this.

Reaching out impulsively, he clutched the curtain in a meaty fist and yanked it open, the clips breaking free and clattering noisely on the deck at his feet.

At the sound, Werner and Inga sat up abruptly on the narrow bunk. Both were still fully clothed, but obviously disheveled. The U-boat captain snarled sleepily, "Goddamn you, Henke, what in hell do you want?"

The general, as surprised as Werner, could only gape wordlessly as he tried to think of some logical excuse for his action. He was saved by the crackling intercom as Werner, now fully awake, realized that the throbbing engine and the fresh air streaming through the ventilators meant the boat was on the surface. Ignoring the general, he glanced at the chronometer on the bulkhead over his desk while Hans's voice called over the static: "Kapitän to the bridge!"

Staggering up, Werner glared angrily at Inga. "When did we surface? Why wasn't I called?"

"You were sleeping so soundly," Inga answered feebly as Werner pushed roughly passed Henke into the corridor, making for the bridge.

The general remained in the doorway, his big fist still balled in the curtain and a lecherous smirk on his face as Inga got up slowly, straightening her hair and clothes.

"So," Henke sneered, "the bitch does make the kapitän's voyage more pleasant than for the rest of us."

Filled with mixed emotions of anger and shame, she avoided his tiny accusing eyes and muttered hoarsely, "Get out! Get out, you pig!"

Werner, storming angrily out on the bridge, saw they were now moving along a wide lead of black water through the brief arctic twilight, but before he could begin chastising his exec for the failure to obey orders, Hans was pointing over the coaming toward the foredeck where an astonishing event was taking place. The Führer was making a speech.

"Jesu, Maria and Josef," Werner breathed.

Bundled to the eyes in his greatcoat and muffler, and speaking as if to the multitudes back in Berlin, Hitler was standing on the foredeck addressing the white expanse of empty ice. There in the gloomy, yellowish twilight, his voice barely audible above the rumbling diesel, the Führer was ranting loudly against Bolshevism and Jewry. To make matters worse, someone had turned on the boat's gramophone to full volume, and the music was coming through the forehatch, sending the strains of Wagner booming across the ice.

"Mein Gott," Inga murmured at Werner's shoulder. He was only then aware that she had joined him on the bridge. "I remember that speech, his final peace offering to Britain in 1940." She stared incredulously at Werner. Hitler was even pausing, as if still hearing the thundering roar of thousands.

One bitter thought was flashing through Werner's mind at that moment, that he had caused the deaths of hundreds because of that man out there. Then he turned to Hans. "Christ, he'll break out in a chorus of the Horst

Wessel song next. Who opened that forward hatch?"

"General Henke ordered one of the seamen."

"Get that son of a bitch up here. And put the sailor on report."

While Hans bent over the voicepipe, Werner and Inga continued to watch the Führer's performance. His antics had always bordered on the ludicrous, but here in this setting it was like a background for Dante's *Inferno* in a deep freeze, a scene of sheer insanity.

Henke's head no sooner appeared in the open hatchway of the bridge behind Werner than the captain verbally lashed out at him, "When are you going to stop giving orders aboard my boat, Henke? Look down there!" He pointed as the general moved to the coaming. "Get that madman back down below!"

Henke reddened, spluttering, "But, I can't. I can't order the Fuhrer."

Werner gripped the general's arm hard. "Listen to me, Henke. Understand me, for all our sakes. I alone give the orders here. And I don't have a brig aboard, but I swear I'll clap him in irons and you along with him if you don't get him off my foredeck now!"

They watched while Henke climbed down the bridge ladder to the deck and shuffled forward along the casing to the end of the rail where he engaged the Führer in conversation. It was quickly evident that Hitler didn't appreciate being interrupted in the middle of a speech. He was soon giving the general seven kinds of hell, and Werner had about decided he was going to have to fire off a flaregun to get their attention when Eva's head appeared in the foredeck hatchway as she climbed out to join them.

Together she and Henke managed to get the Führer calmed and finally back down below. Someone shut off the gramophone, and Werner sent one of the lookouts down on the foredeck to close and secure the hatch behind them. Then he turned to Hans. "Now that's done, my standing order was that I be called before surfacing through any open leads, Oberleutnant. Why was that order disobeyed?"

"But you were called, Herr K'leu," Hans answered calmly.

"Yes, Werner," Inga spoke up, confirming it, "you were called. But I shut off the intercom. You were sleeping so deeply," she blushed, "so peacefully, I didn't want to awaken you."

Werner's angry retort died before it left his lips. She was a woman and a civilian. Besides, his military authority meant little anymore. He was still the captain of a ship at sea, and his orders were to be obeyed, but he wasn't all that sure of his decisions anymore. He had been refreshed by the interlude, and Hans was certainly competent enough for command. Hadn't Werner recommended him for a boat of his own a good six months before the war's end? He looked at them both and smiled uneasily. "If I don't manage to kill us all before this voyage is over, you two will."

"Ice, K'leu!" a lookout suddenly shouted, pointing. And there, a hundred meters ahead of their bow the solid ice was closing. The wind had shifted and was blowing in their faces, hurling the sharp ice particles like stinging sand. Suddenly the frozen jaws of the lead were snapping shut with a dull booming sound like thunder.

Werner stepped to the voicepipe. "Dead slow ahead," he ordered. As the engine telegraph jangled down below he wondered if there would be time to sit awhile on the surface and continue the charge. "How much juice have we got, Chief?"

"Seventy per cent, K'leu."

"And oil?"

"Sixty-two tons."

Already the twilight was gone and the flat arctic daylight strong again. But the overcast was heavy, and a fog bank was rolling up ahead of them. There was no sign of where the sun might be to get a position line.

Hans seemed to read his mind. "A large part of the sky cleared just as twilight began, K'leu," he said, barely able to suppress a proud smile as he glanced at the figures in his notebook. "Allowing for distortions, we're at approximately 74-10 North and 91-20 West. Somerset Island is eighteen miles off our port beam. Devon about the same distance to the north. Viscount Melville Sound is less than two hundred miles over the bow."

Werner wished he could share some of the optimism of his exec, but even with the port engine returned to service by Horst's makeshift bearings, and a seventy per cent charge for the motors, the starboard diesel had now begun to knock ominously. He knew that two hundred miles over the bow could still be forever.

He took a deep breath and looked warmly at them both. "Let's take one obstacle at a time," he said, "and right now it's the shallow narrows of Barrow Strait with the ice closing fast around us. Clear the bridge, Hans. Stand by to dive."

SEVENTEEN

"Jesu, Maria and Josef," Werner's lips formed a half prayer, half curse as their troubles rapidly mounted. For one thing he had begun to think that all of the Barrow Strait was roofed over solidly with ice. In thirty-two hours of submerged running they had found only two small breathing holes where they had managed to blow up against the ice and raise the snort mast long enough to top off the batteries and air. Then with the juice almost exhausted, and the air in the boat stale and leaden again, the break had come, a real opening in the eternal ice, and emergence into the eastern end of the vast Viscount Melville Sound.

But they had surfaced in no ordinary lead. Standing now on the bridge with Hans and Inga and the lookouts under a thick overcast amid swirling wisps of fog, they surveyed the frigid white world around them and listened to the distant grinding, booming and thundering of restless floes that could be heard even above the rough rumbling of the port diesel as it put on the charge.

Instead of a watery lead through the ice, they appeared to be in a wide melt full of brash and block and floating islands of ice that varied in size from small flat pans to huge glistening hulks the size of houses.

Cautiously, Werner called down the changes in their heading to the helmsman and held the boat's speed to six knots as they maneuvered among the loose and dangerous ice. To make matters worse they were now so close to the magnetic pole that it was difficult to maintain any kind of adjustment on the compasses or the gyro.

Hans, studying the chart, took a bearing off Young Island, which rose out of the ice a few hundred meters off their stern. Werner was relieved that they were at least into the sound. Surely they couldn't miss the broad mouth of McClure Strait at the western end.

But in the next twelve hours more problems developed. Forced under again after only two hours on the surface, the port motor switchboard that had caught fire two days before finally malfunctioned completely. The technicians began tearing it down and practically rewiring the whole thing. When they found the sound open enough to surface again, the water-cooling pump went out on the starboard diesel and the clutch failed. Horst and a machinist were busy adapting the reversing clutch to forward drive.

All this left them in a precarious situation at best, and Werner didn't like to think what might happen if they were forced to dive again anytime soon. At least the jury-rigged bearings in the port engine were holding. He was about to wonder aloud what in hell else could go wrong when it did. The muttering port diesel stopped abruptly, and the sudden silence closed around them like a white velvet glove.

Reacting instantly, Werner crossed the bridge and cupped a mittened hand around the voicepipe. "Chief?" he called.

"Bushing's busted, K'leu," Horst's voice came back almost immediately. The U-boat was already losing way, and Werner quickly called a course correction to avoid a drifting berg even as his mind raced desperately. Glancing at Hans he saw that even his exec's usually invincible optimism seemed to be wavering. Then Horst's voice came up the pipe again. "We've started repairs on the bushing, K'leu."

"That will take hours," Werner answered. "What about the clutch on the starboard diesel?"

"Another two hours at least on that, K'leu."

"Stay with it," Werner ordered and once more looked around them at the ice giants looming on all sides. If they suddenly started closing, they still had the starboard motor.

"Can't we just submerge without power?" Inga wondered aloud. "And simply hover beneath the ice until the repairs are made?"

Werner shook his head. "A U-boat can't hover, at least not in the sense you're thinking. With her negative buoyancy she's not even a true submersible, and without powered seaway on the hydroplanes they can't hold us suspended in the water. We'd sink to the bottom, and the bottom is some two hundred fathoms beneath us along here." He was looking at Hans as he spoke, and realizing his exec was having the same thoughts, he added hopefully, "But what we might do is go deep enough to maybe find a layer of heavy water to sit on. If not that, at least we could try and hold the boat above crush depth and beneath the ice by alternately flooding and blowing her tanks while repairs are made, or until we run out of compressed air."

"It sounds dangerous either way," Inga said, "and I think there's a way to stay on the surface safely." She looked hesitantly at them both. "Or at least with relative safety."

Both Werner and Hans were willing to listen as she pointed toward the ice surrounding them and explained her solution. "I've been studying the ice. We're in a large melt again, like a lake, and the set of the drift is westerly. All the ice is moving in the same direction at the same speed. If you could anchor your ship to one of the bergs and simply drift with the flow, you wouldn't need engine power to outmaneuver it, at least as long as the melt holds out."

Werner exchanged glances with Hans, and the exec was suddenly his old beaming optimistic self. "It ought to work, K'leu. At least I'd say it's a better chance than we'd have down below."

Werner considered his alternatives only briefly. A man made many choices in life, and he'd found that most were irreversible. He knew that whenever a U-boat captain made a wrong one, it almost always was his last. But he'd never shied away from necessary snap decisions before and he made one now. "We'll do it," he said almost defiantly.

Minutes later he had picked out a medium size berg and ordered the starboard motor started just long enough to bring them alongside where sailors secured the boat with long lines dipped in the water and then allowed to freeze to the ice fore and aft. Werner then had them stand by with hand axes, ready to chop the lines free in an emergency.

He had already ordered all nonessential auxiliary machinery shut off again to save what little juice they still had, including the heaters. He knew it was about time for the general to make an appearance.

It didn't take long for Henke's ruddy features to appear

in the hatchway. Blustering furiously and just a little drunk, he flourished a half-empty schnapps bottle as he pulled himself out on the bridge and demanded to know why the heaters had been shut off again.

"Guten morgen, Herr General," Werner greeted him pleasantly. "I've been expecting you."

"The heaters, goddammit, what's happened to the verdammte heaters?"

"I've ordered them turned off temporarily. We have a problem, Herr General. Haven't you noticed the stillness?"

With remarkable restraint but growing satisfaction, Werner explained their dangerous predicament and the alternatives open to them, watching the general's face dissolve in sheer terror as he only now seemed to notice the looming iceberg they had moored themselves to. Henke actually seemed to shrink deeper inside his greatcoat as he whispered horrified, "Gott en Himmel, we are lost!"

"Not necessarily," Werner answered dryly. "But I think you've had enough of this." Taking the bottle from the general's hand, he hurled it over the side where it smashed against the face of the berg, leaving a broad yellow stain that spread slowly over the ice. "Now you will return below, Herr General, and you will advise the Führer and his wife that the heaters will be turned on again as soon as one of the engines is repaired and we can put a charge on the batteries. But that will be several hours away."

Surprisingly sobered now, Henke simply nodded contritely and turning, let himself awkwardly down the hatch.

Werner turned to Inga and Hans. "The next few hours will tell. Relieve the men at those lines every hour, Exec."

"Jawohl, K'leu."

"And you'd better tell the cook to make plenty of hot soup for lunch, and to get some more coffee up here now."

"Jawohl, K'leu," Hans grinned and moved to the voicepipe.

Werner looked at Inga. "It'll be as cold down below as up here soon, but at least the air temperature is barely at freezing and there's not much wind. I'd estimate our speed of drift at about three knots." Then he stared up at the scudding clouds. "A sudden weather change might be our biggest worry. The barometer is falling. So for the moment I'd say we're in the hands of whatever ice devils might be abroad."

"I feel a lot safer when we're just in your capable hands, Werner," she answered softly. "I think—"

"K'leu!" One of the lookouts was pointing through the rail of the wintergarten toward the stern, and both Werner and Inga looked back in time to see one of the sailors steady himself on the mooring line as he stepped down on the saddle tank, axe in hand, and killed a curious seal that had poked its head around a side of the berg.

A second sailor stepped down to help his mate. When the two men had heaved the bloodied carcass up on the casing, Werner ordered two sailors up on deck to butcher it. "See what the cook can do with it," he told them, and looked at Inga. "It should be enough to make a fresh stew for everyone, and a welcome change of diet." Then he called down to the sailor who had killed the seal, "Just don't try that with a polar bear, Dietrich, or he'll be the one having a change of diet!"

Three hours later Werner was alone on the bridge with the lookouts when an electrical artificer reported that the port motor switchboard was repaired. So at least they had both motors again, but still very little juice to run them. Horst reported that another hour or so was needed before the bushing would be replaced, although the repair of the water-cooling pump and adaption of the reversing clutch on the starboard engine would be accomplished soon.

But would it be soon enough, Werner was wondering, cupping his mittened hands around a thick mug of steaming coffee and watching the lookouts drinking theirs while they stared steadfastly into the swirling fog and listened to the dull booming sounds of the ice that had started again, this time from the south.

Their rate of drift had slowed until any movement was hardly noticeable now. They seemed suspended like a ghost ship amid the pale, gossamer veils of fog and the solidly frozen bergs around them. In the periods of stillness between the distant cracking and thundering of the ice, they could hear the faint metallic clinks from deep in the boat where the machinists were making their repairs.

Then the ethereal serenity was broken by the harsh rasping squeal of steel as the hatch on the foredeck was pushed open, and Werner, stepping to the coaming, looked down wonderingly as a sailor emerged and then helped the figure of the Führer out on deck. "Verdammte Scheisse!" Werner swore openly. "Not another speech!" And he was about to move to the voicepipe but stopped.

Hitler was merely standing there by the open hatch, gazing around. He looked first at the two seamen standing by the forward lines, then up at the awesome height of the glittering greenish berg they were tied to. Then his gaze moved upward toward the bridge of the U-boat. For a long moment his pale and pasty face, drawn and shrunken like a skull's, fixed firmly on Werner's.

A moment later he had turned away, and without a word he let the sailor help him back down the hatch. The sailor followed him, closing the hatch behind them with the same grating screech of metal.

The bow lookouts glanced curiously at Werner, but said nothing as behind them Hans Pohl pulled himself up out of the bridge hatch and stepped to the coaming beside the captain. "Henke says the Führer has come up on deck again," he said. "He says he couldn't stop him."

Werner shook his head. "He's already gone back down."

"What, no speeches?" Hans asked wryly.

"No speeches," Werner answered somberly. The ghastly expression on Hitler's face had shaken him. "In fact," he added, "I've never seen such a look of outright hopelessness and despair in a man."

Hans pulled off his gloves and blew thoughtfully on his fingers. "We will make it, K'leu," he said slowly. "We will raise McClure Strait and the Arctic Ocean beyond, and the Bering Strait and Japan. We will do it, K'leu."

"Will we, Hans?"

A sudden muffled explosion down below momentarily startled them both. The lookouts glanced around, and the sailors standing by the lines looked up towards the bridge. But the boat, the berg and the fog drifted serenely on, a unified entity seemingly undisturbed.

Werner had even begun to wonder if they had all imagined it when a second muffled roar echoed up from below and the captain, turning the conn over to Hans, plunged down the hatch, dropping off the ladder into the control room and a mass of confusion.

A sailor was pointing through the forward hatchway. Werner climbed through and hurried along the aisle and through the wardroom and officers' mess where he found Henke and Inga and several others gathered in front of the forward torpedo room.

Chief Petty Officer Bruno Haupmann nodded toward the closed hatch of the Führer's quarters and muttered hoarsely, "Gunshots, K'leu, from in there."

EIGHTEEN

For a moment no one seemed to know what to do next. Then Werner nodded at the chief petty officer. "Open it, Haupmann."

"Jawohl, K'leu." Grasping the wheel on the heavy door, Haupmann turned it and pulled it open as the thought struck Werner that it was oddly like opening an ancient tomb.

When Bruno Haupmann stepped out of the way, Werner moved to the opening and peered inside while the others crowded around him. It was the first time he had looked into the forward compartment since the official party had come aboard. The scene was not exactly inspiring.

In the dim lighting, amid the normal clutter of human occupancy in close quarters, even the pretense of elegance had almost vanished. The once plush carpeting that covered the deck plates and the ornate tapestry adorning the bulk heads were swollen with damp and mold.

But what caught and held his gaze were the bodies of Hitler and his wife, still bundled in their greatcoats and lying crumpled beside the double-tiered bunks, the darkly glistening stains of blood pooled and already congealing on the carpet under them. The compartment reeked of cordite fumes, and a P-38 Walther pistol lay in the Führer's outstretched hand.

Werner, stepping inside, knelt and felt for a pulse in the Führer's neck, then Eva's. There was none. He hadn't expected any, since the woman had been shot in the temple and Hitler had put the pistol barrel in his mouth, leaving a bunk post sprayed with blood and bone and brains.

Moving quickly back to the hatchway, Werner looked around at the stunned faces of Henke and Inga and the others as they drew away from the opening. His eyes found the boat's medic and he motioned to him. "Kranz—inside—verify with me that they are dead."

"Please, no, K'leu," the medic cringed away. "Please, I—"

"Someone has to, Kranz," Werner told him gently but firmly. "And you're qualified. Quickly now, it's an order."

It took only moments for Kranz to enter the compartment and confirm the murder-suicide. "Both dead from gunshots, K'leu," he reported stiffly, and Werner looked out at Henke. "Herr General? Do you wish to examine the bodies?"

But Henke too shrank back, shaking his head. "No—no," he whispered, horrified, his whole expression full of shocked disbelief.

Well, thought Werner in the midst of an awkward silence, what now?

Then he decided. Turning around, he moved passed Kranz and the two bodies to the forward end of the compartment where he reached up and grasped the priceless Turkish tapestry and yanked it down, exposing the glistening cold steel doors of the torpedo tubes.

Glancing back at the chief petty officer who was still

waiting with Henke outside the hatchway, he ordered, "Haupmann, have the cargo removed from one of these tubes and put the bodies inside for now." Climbing back out of the compartment, he looked at Henke again. "Any objections, Herr General?"

"No," Henke shook his head slowly, his voice still barely audible, his gaze cloudy as if still in shock.

"Very well then." Werner looked around at the others. "The Führer and his wife are dead, but we're committed to this voyage now, so everyone will resume his duties. Verstanden?" And making his way back along the gangway and into the control room, he stepped to the chart table and re-examined their plot, more to give himself something to do and a chance to think than to see where they were going.

Aware now that Inga and the general had entered the control room behind him, he turned and voiced his thoughts, reiterating that the voyage must continue, if for no other reason than they had progressed too far, expended too much fuel to turn back now. There was no way out but to continue pushing westward through the ice.

General Henke was staring at him. "Or south, Kapitän," he said somberly.

"South?"

"I too can read a chart, Reutemann," Henke continued arrogantly, his horror at the death of his Führer apparently overcome. "To the southwest is the large land mass of Victoria Island, and south of that the Canadian mainland—"

"Which is still hundreds of miles from civilization," Werner interrupted him. "And you propose a journey across the ice of this land mass on foot? You're as mad as

Karl was, Henke."

"And I tell you, Reutemann, it is this voyage that is madness. There is no purpose now to accomplish, no reason to continue west. I was talking to some of your men even before the Führer's death—"

Werner's sudden dangerous expression stopped him. "What do you mean, General, you've been talking to my men? I told you what would happen if you tried to give any more orders."

Henke drew back under Werner's angry gaze. "I was merely discussing other possibilities. Surely you don't really think you can still get this pig-boat through the western ice—why it's not even running!"

As if to belie his words, Horst Wolff suddenly poked his red-whiskered face through the stern hatchway and announced, "Reversing clutch is adapted to forward drive, K'leu. The water-cooling pump's repaired. Want me to crank up the starboard engine and start the charge?"

"The sooner the better, Chief," Werner answered, smiling triumphantly at Henke. "We can't stay anchored to this old berg forever." Motioning for Inga to follow him, he led her up the conning tower ladder.

"Will we free ourselves from that berg now?" she asked as they climbed to the upper hatch.

"Not yet, at least not as long as this westerly drift and the weather both hold. I want Horst to start the charge and check out that engine thoroughly, and maybe even get the port diesel running too, before we give up our free ride."

Even as they emerged out on the bridge, the starboard engine coughed twice, belching smoke, then came roaring to life and began to idle noisely while putting on the charge. The lookouts on the bridge and the seamen standing by the lines fore and aft cheered, and Hans Pohl began slapping his gloved hands together and stamping his feet for warmth. "So, K'leu," he grinned, "we have hope once more." Then his expression grew serious. "But we are without our illustrious passengers."

Werner glanced at the lookouts and then back at his exec. "You heard what happened?"

Hans nodded. "Horst called me on the voicepipe. It is just as well, K'leu. But what will we do with the bodies?"

"Haupmann is putting them in one of the tubes for now. I'll have to decide whether to bury them at sea or try to carry them with us to Japan. It's certainly cold enough for them to keep." He was looking around at the bleak, gray day. The fog had lifted and visibility was at least a thousand meters as they continued their westerly drift with the brash and block. But the overcast had lowered considerably, and the temperature was falling. With the engine putting on the charge now, he decided to have the heaters started again before they had to chop the ice off the chart table.

He had just crossed the bridge to give the order on the voicepipe when Bruno Haupmann's voice came up from below: "Kapitän to the forward torpedo room!"

What now, Werner thought as he left Hans and Inga on the bridge. He got his answer as the sailors who had gathered around the open hatch gave way to let him through. He looked inside the compartment. The bodies of Hitler and his wife still lay side by side on the bloodied carpet. One of the heavy wooden cargo crates had been removed from the number four tube and stacked neatly in one corner. But one had not, and the petty officers and sailors were all staring down at this second crate, which

147

obviously had been dropped.

Breaking open, it had spilled nearly half its contents onto the carpeted deck. There they lay, gleaming in the dim light, yellow bars of gold bullion tumbled beside bundles of securities and currencies from half a dozen countries—American dollars, Swiss francs, British pounds. And jewels, glittering, dazzling precious stones of every kind and description.

And there were seven more such crates aboard.

NINETEEN

Standing there with the others in the forward torpedo room, it was like gazing down at a Pharaoh's secret treasure horde. Once again the discomforting analogy of a tomb crossed Werner's mind.

But thinking about it, he wondered why he should be so surprised. Had he really thought that the eight crates loaded at Bergen and stowed in the forward tubes had really been simply the Führer's personal belongings. Eight heavy, metal-banded wooden crates? The truth was he hadn't thought about it at all. He had accepted them at face value. There had been so many other things to think about.

Now that he did think about it, and if the rest of the crates contained a similar amount of Nazi loot, then the total wealth he was carrying in his forward tubes was indeed a Pharaoh's ransom and staggering to imagine. Certainly enough to continue the Nazi movement—or perhaps start a new republican Germany on the road to recovery.

Looking around he ordered the compartment cleared except for Bruno Haupmann and his work party. He then had them repack the broken end of the crate, carefully nail it shut again, and stack it in the corner with the other one they had already removed.

When the bodies had been consigned to the number four tube and the door closed, Werner moved with the others out of the compartment and personally closed and secured the hatch behind them. Then he ordered a guard posted around the clock. "No one is to enter the compartment except on my personal order, Haupmann, understood?"

"Jawohl, Herr K'leu. No one."

Back in the control room Werner knew there was no way to stop this latest news from spreading throughout the boat. He got on the intercom and announced what he hoped was a reasonable explanation of the unusual circumstances. "With the Führer dead," he told them, "we don't know what the exact legal status of his property will be when we reach Japan. Even the status of our German government is uncertain at best. But," he reminded them, "we know we are still Germans. It remains our duty, our sacred trust, to reach our ally with what we have.

"This may be all there is to rebuild our beloved country, and we will accept our duty as we always have, in the loyal spirit of national honor that has always been the tradition of the Deutsche Kriegsmarine. That is all."

Climbing through the tower back up to the bridge, he found Hans and Inga standing by the periscopes. The four lookouts had their glasses to their eyes as the drift continued amid the raucous idling of the diesel putting on the charge. "You heard it up here?" Werner asked his exec and Inga.

They both nodded. "Word of the crate's contents just came up with the change of watch," Inga said.

"Will we take the bodies all the way to Japan too, K'leu?" Hans asked.

"I suppose we'll have to." He was gazing around at the bleakness of the ice and the hazy, sunless day. "Who would believe us otherwise?"

"Werner," Inga said, "didn't you know what was in those cargo crates? Didn't you at least suspect?"

Werner smiled whimsically. "Would you believe I actually thought they were the Führer's personal effects? They could have been stamped INDUSTRIAL MACHINE PARTS or EVA'S DOILIES or GOLD in big red letters for that matter. I just wasn't paying them that much attention, even though Kommandant Voss was. There were just too many other things on my mind at the time. Anyway, we've got the treasure now, and the responsibility that goes with it."

"We've also got a suddenly strangely reticent SS officer," Hans noted, nodding behind them toward the wintergarten where General Henke was leaning heavily on the rail and staring aft toward a gathering fog bank.

Three hours later Horst Wolff reported a sixty per cent charge on the batteries and the air tanks filled, with the starboard diesel performing well and repairs to the port engine now complete. And almost simultaneously Hans called down from the bridge, "We're losing the melt, K'leu! Solid ice dead ahead!"

Climbing back up on the bridge, Werner looked at the icebound sea that was rapidly appearing over the bow. Behind them the fog bank had deepened and was less than a hundred meters away now, with a freshening wind and the sky from horizon to horizon a sullen, sunless gray.

The sounds of booming, grinding ice had begun again, and they weren't too far away now. "Cut loose the lines!" Werner called to the men standing by on the casings fore and aft. Moving to the voicepipe he ordered, "Chief, shift from the starboard engine to port. Give it a check run and then go on the port motor. We're running out of seaway up ahead."

Under their own power again, and with the weather rapidly deteriorating, Werner called down course changes to the helmsman as the U-boat slowly eased away from the berg and gradually increased speed to seven knots. As they began threading their way among the brash and block and thickening slush, Inga's face appeared in the open hatch as she pulled up the furred hood of her anorak. "How far do you think it is now to McClure Strait?" she asked.

Werner looked at Hans, who had made the last dead reckoning on their drift.

"We've only made about seventy-five miles in the past twenty-four hours by my estimate," Hans said, "leaving us still a couple of hundred miles from McClure."

"Come up, Inga," Werner helped her out on the bridge and then pointed with his binoculars over the bow again. "What's it look like to you? The ice should be getting looser, but instead it seems to be thickening."

Inga had stepped to the coaming and was gazing intently at the ice and sky. When she looked at Werner again, she was frowning. "It doesn't look good, any of it. The weather should be better this time of year. And the ice," she shook her head, "with that kind up ahead, McClure just might be impassable—deep drift ice and few open leads. Remember, it jams up there coming down from the pole, and it's been known to stay icebound all year long."

Werner nodded. "Then maybe we'd better head further south and find Prince of Wales Strait along the east coast of Banks Island."

Inga agreed. "It's narrower and shallower, but there should be less ice, or at least more open leads."

"If we can find the entrance," Hans suggested, suddenly uncharacteristically cynical. He too was frowning now. "Our last navigation fix was that bearing off Young Island. Unless we've misjudged the speed or direction of our drift, we should be about a quarter of the way through the sound. But it's a good eighty miles wide here, and the only thing I'm sure of is that we are somewhere in the middle of it, because we've got over two hundred fathoms under our keel."

"Well," Werner smiled faintly, "don't tell Henke. He worries too much as it is." He said it facetiously, but it was more to cover his own deepening concern. With only some sixty tons of fuel in the bunkers, they couldn't afford many exploratory side trips.

"And where is our illustrious general?" Hans wanted to know.

"He was talking with several of the crew in the wardroom a few minutes ago," Inga said. "But they grew abruptly quiet as I passed through."

Werner glanced curiously at Hans.

"Henke trying to give orders again?" the exec wondered aloud.

"If he is, it'll be the last time," Werner said, wiping the lenses of his binoculars and taking one last look at the heavy weather ahead. "I'll put that rogue in irons without another word said." He lowered the glasses and looked around at Hans. "Prepare to dive."

"Clear the bridge," Hans ordered, then stepped to the voicepipe. "Diving stations!" And he followed Inga and the lookouts down the hatch.

With the fog closing in and the resonant thundering of

the ice beginning again, Werner took a last look around. The same thought brushed his mind, as always, the wonder if this time might be his last look at the sky. Then he too climbed down the tower ladder and secured the hatch wheel over their heads.

"Flood," he ordered, dropping into the control room. The chief engineer signaled the planesmen and the technicians at the hydraulic valves. "Down to thirty meters."

As the water rushed into the tanks and the planesmen leaned into their wheels, the U-boat tilted forward in a shallow angle of dive with her port motor humming. Werner stood braced behind the planesmen, watching the gauges and dials over their heads.

But as Horst gave orders to level off and trim the boat at thirty meters, a slight tingle of foreboding, a sensing that something somewhere was not quite right, barely touched Werner when the bow planesman reported, "Dive planes jammed, sir!"

The U-boat was suddenly plummeting unchecked toward the bottom some two hundred fathoms below.

TWENTY

"Blow all tanks," Werner ordered calmly in a desperate effort to halt the dive. "Hard rise on stern planes. Shift bow planes to manual control." But while compressed air shrieked into the diving tanks, one of the technicians mistakenly opened a flooding valve instead of tripping a blowing lever, and Werner watched the depth gauge needle flicker past sixty meters as the boat continued falling.

The chief himself made the correction, cursing. With the bow planes finally operating manually and set on full rise, and with the air pushing the water out of the ballast tanks, he was able to catch the boat at a hundred twenty-seven meters where her old plates began protesting again, creaking and groaning under the pressure. Several oil and water lines started leaking.

"Get us back up and trimmed out at sixty meters, Chief," Werner ordered, "then have a little talk with that rating. And get someone working on those bow planes."

"Jawohl, K'leu."

Then, ignoring the rising depth gauge, Werner turned to the chart table where he began working with the dividers and parallel rules, as worried now about their true position as about the continuing mechanical failures of the boat.

Hans's estimate that they were at least still in the middle of Viscount Melville Sound due to the extreme depth of the water under them was true enough, but where in the sound? It was a vast body of water and ice, and with their charts of the area lacking so much detail, even navigating by radar was useless.

And how accurate was their estimate of drift or any of their dead reckoning for that matter? With no known land bearings or radio beacons, and with no recent celestial fix, they could be almost anywhere west of the Barrow Strait and east of McClure. Dammit, he thought, they needed some time on the surface with a clear sky. Otherwise, he knew they could easily miss even the wide mouth of McClure by miles, let alone finding the narrow entrance to the Prince of Wales Strait.

"Boat trimmed out at sixty meters, K'leu," Horst Wolff reported as Werner felt the lurch and heard the gurgle of water in the trim tanks. Then the chief added quietly, "We're picking up speed, K'leu. We're making over ten knots while our rpm's remain the same."

Werner looked around, then glanced at the gauges, dials and the gyrocompass. "We've picked up an undersea current," he said, "a southwesterly current. Slow to one and one-half knots, Chief, just enough to maintain way on the planes. Let's ride it as long as it continues westerly."

For the next eight hours they rode the swift undersea current westward, deep beneath the ice. Werner knew he should have been seeking out such hidden currents all along, saving both the batteries and their diesel fuel, and he berated himself for not thinking of it instead of having to stumble on it accidentally.

It also gave Fritz Oder a much needed rest. The strain of keeping the boat away from the overhead ice yet close enough to find the vital open leads was becoming to much for his nervous system. Werner had relieved him with the less qualified Adolph Schmidt as often as he could, but the man's nerves were frayed.

His own nerves weren't all that great, he reflected moodily, and now he couldn't find one of the charts, the one covering the southern part of the sound and the vast land mass to the south that was Victoria Island. He turned to his exec across the control room. "Hans, did you move one of the charts?"

"No, K'leu."

"Well, somebody did. It's missing."

For a moment there was only an awkward silence in the control room. The hum of the port motor and the auxiliary machinery seemed uncommonly loud. Then the chief engineer spoke up. "I can explain the missing chart, K'leu."

Werner looked at him, puzzled. "Please do."

But before Horst could explain anything, Inga's stricken voice startled them all. "Werner!"

They turned to find her pale, pain-stricken face in the forward hatchway. Her arm was held twisted behind her back by General Henke who was right behind her and who also held his P-38 Walther pistol against the back of her neck.

"No hostile moves, Kapitän," Henke ordered tersely, a dangerously wild desperation obvious in his eyes and voice. "Not from anyone. Don't even twitch. Not if you wish her to live." Quickly, he shifted the pistol around to the front, tucking the barrel up under her jaw and keeping her in front of him while maneuvering her backwards until both of them were in a corner of the control room. Three sailors climbed quickly through the hatchway after them. One of them was armed with a short crowbar, and another with a long-bladed hunting knife, honed to a keen edge.

"What in hell is this, Henke?" Werner demanded, though he knew damn well what it was: mutiny. The general was obviously over the edge. But it was evidently a deliberate and planned assault, and in the anxiety of the last few hours Werner had been so occupied once again with the boat that he had forgotten about the general, and about Inga's mentioning his mysterious meeting with some of the crew. It was an oversight he was now regretting desperately himself.

"We are taking over your ship, Kapitän," Henke was saying, nodding to the three men who had entered with him. They were Kern, Berchtold and Meyer, all seamen and part of the off-duty watch. "You will also relieve Godt and Schulz there at the dive planes," Henke continued, "and Adolph Schmidt at the fathometer."

"I see," Werner said carefully, fighting for control of his churning emotions. For a moment he took his eyes off Henke's pistol and the trigger finger pressed so close against Inga's ashen face and stared at the mutineers. But none of them would meet their captain's hard glare of outrage.

"You'd also better send for your second engineer, Reutemann," Henke said tightly. "Your friend, Horst Wolff, also has other duties now."

"You goddamned fool!" Horst blurted, swearing a thick Bavarian oath as his ruddy face grew redder by the second. He clenched and unclenched the fist of his uninjured arm. "Now is not the time, Henke! You've acted too soon!"

"We could wait no longer," the general told him coldly. "One more mechanical or human failure like the last and we will all be on the bottom. We're going now as soon as we can find another opening in the ice." He looked back at Werner. "Now relieve those men, Reutemann."

But Werner and Hans were both staring in disbelief at their chief engineer. "Horst?" Werner asked incredulously. He could not have been more shocked if Hans had turned on him. And the chief's suddenly nervous, sheepish look couldn't hold the captain's hurt, accusing eyes.

"I'm sorry, K'leu," Horst said gruffly, miserably, lowering his gaze. "I offer no excuse. I simply had to choose, and I chose to be practical. The general is right about the failures of the boat. Our only chance is to abandon it, take what we can, and head south. I knew you would never agree."

Werner's slow smile was empty, joyless. "And by 'taking what you can' you of course mean the treasure crates?"

"Of course we mean the treasure!" Henke interrupted them. "Now get your second up here, and replacements for these technicians. Then get on the intercom and inform the rest of the crew who is in command and what the consequences will be for any attempts at heroism."

Again Werner and Horst exchanged glances. "He means it, K'leu," Horst said and shrugged. "For us the voyage is over. We have studied the chart. If we can get ashore on Victoria Island, we can make our way overland to some Eskimo settlement on the south coast."

"But that's some three hundred miles over the ice on foot!" Werner protested, still incredulous that this was really happening. "And how do you propose to transport eight heavy crates?"

"One crate, K'leu," Horst corrected him. "One will be enough for us—Herr Henke has agreed—and we'll jury-rig runners from the bunk rails and make a sled of the crate itself, with our supplies tied on top. The men will trade off towing it. When we reach a settlement, we'll steal a boat for the trip across Coronation Gulf. Once in the Canadian Northwest Territories, we'll divide the loot and every man will be on his own. It's a good plan, K'leu. The best we've got."

"It's a fool's plan!" Werner was shaking his head. "You're as mad as he is, Horst."

"Not mad, K'leu, desperate. Now do as the general says. Give the orders—please."

Glancing once more at the pistol barrel tucked tightly under Inga's jaw, Werner stepped to the intercom and ordered the second engineer and three off-duty technicians to the control room. Then he advised the rest of the crew of Henke's takeover. He also advised them that all orders would henceforth be coming from the general, and that there would be instant obedience or a lot of deaths, beginning with Frau Brandt whom Henke now held hostage. Finished, he turned to the general. "Satisfied?"

"That will do for now, Kapitän. Now if we can have your own pistol and the one the Führer used, I think that will account for all the small arms known to be aboard."

"I threw the Führer's into the sea. Horst saw me do it. My own is in my locker, a Luger."

Henke glanced at Kern who was holding the crowbar. "You and Berchtold go break it open."

"No need for that," Werner said, reaching cautiously into his pocket and producing a key. "Here." He held it out to Kern. As soon as the two sailors disappeared through the forward hatch, three more entered the control room from aft, followed by the second engineer, Jürgen Heuser.

While the technicians relieved their counterparts who had joined the mutineers, Jürgen, with his one good eye, glared in tight-lipped anger and dismay at Horst.

"The Herr General has found seven traitors among us, Jürgen," Werner told him, "so it looks like you're the chief now. Take us up to twenty meters and we'll try for another open lead. Our friends want to trek south across the ice."

"It's very thin ice overhead, K'leu," Fritz Oder, who had taken over from Schmidt, reported only minutes later. "Ice free open water now, K'leu," he continued. "We're under a lead."

Werner glanced at Henke who ordered, "Surface, Kapitän. Gets us up top now!"

Werner looked at Jürgen and nodded. "Take her up, Chief. Blow forward. Blow aft. Hard rise on the planes." While Jürgen signaled the technicians, a thousand thoughts kept tumbling through Werner's mind at this savage turn of events.

What he found most devastating of all was Inga's deadly predicament, and though he was appalled by an acute and unfamiliar sense of helplessness, he tried to look reassuringly once more at her pale and frightened face.

The loss of part of the Nazi treasure meant little to him. Even the possible loss of his boat and the failure of the voyage itself were only secondary now. Because for Werner Reutemann, grappling with a confusing turmoil of worry and fury within, concern was suddenly focused on only one thing, Inga Brandt's safety, her very survival. This and this alone was uppermost in his swirling thoughts.

But at the moment he couldn't think of a thing more he could do to insure it.

TWENTY-ONE

Streaming water off her rust-streaked, dazzle-striped tower and scattering small chunks of ice in all directions, Werner's U-boat heaved up onto the surface of the lead and rode low in the water, her port motor humming and her decks awash. As the upper hatch flew open, men appeared in the horseshoe of the bridge, gazing around them at the bleak arctic day and the same low, thick cloud cover from horizon to horizon. With the temperature standing at thirty-four degrees, the wind out of the north-northwest at five knots was scattering the tufts of fog.

General Henke and Horst Wolff and the other six mutineers, the latter armed now with Werner's Luger as well as the knife and crowbars, would have been no match against the fury of the captain and the rest of his crew, except for the fact that Henke had never released his hold on Inga Brandt.

Even now she was standing beside him, a rope looped around her waist and over Henke's shoulder, his pistol barrel pressed against her ribs. Horst and two of the mutineers were on the bridge with them, while on the railed platform of the wintergarten Werner and Hans waited in impotent anger. The captain couldn't be sure Henke would kill her if they tried to jump him. It would mean his own life too. But Werner knew that with a fool like Henke, he couldn't take the chance.

While Horst called down course corrections to the helmsman in the tower, the U-boat swung south, her starboard engine rumbling as she plowed through the loose ice of the wide lead, seeking the shore. Two of the heavy treasure crates, already fitted with runners made from bunk rails, were hauled up through the hatch on the foredeck. This was over Horst's loud protests that it would be too tiring for six men to pull two heavy sleds with no one to relieve them.

But Henke's greed had overcome what little common sense he possessed. "We'll move slowly," he told Horst, "and there'll be twice as much to share."

They had fashioned snowgoggles of leather strips slitted and tied with boot strings for use against the ice glare, but Werner wondered how they were going to maintain a southerly route with only an unreliable handheld compass.

Then supplies—tinned meat and fruit and bread, along with blankets and a heavy tarpaulin for shelter—were hauled up through the foredeck hatch and lashed over the tops of the crate-sleds. Maneuvering at last close against the icy bank, Horst had the sailors snake out long anchor lines fore and aft and work a gangplank across while he climbed down himself and inspected the crate-sleds.

"Why haven't you asked Inga what she thinks of your scheme, Henke?" Werner shouted suddenly from the wintergarten. "She's the ice expert, the only one of us who's been in this area before. Ask her what your chances are out there on the ice!"

Surprisingly, instead of answering, Henke untied the rope and simply released her, shoving her into the wintergarten toward Werner and Hans while still holding his pistol trained on the three of them. As she staggered forward into Werner's arms, he caught and held her, hardly able to believe the man had actually freed her.

"Your whore's opinions don't impress me, Kapitän!" Henke shouted back viciously. "She would only lie anyway, so I'm going to have the pleasure of personally executing all three of you before we leave!" He raised the Walther to chest level.

"Wait!" Horst Wolff had climbed back up to the bridge. Reaching across the periscope standard he tried to grab Henke's arm, but the other two mutineers standing beside the general moved in time to block the engineer's way.

Henke glared at Horst angrily. "Be careful, Leutnant, you'll spoil my aim. Perhaps you can understand now why I didn't trust you with the other pistol."

"Goddammit, General use your head!" Horst yelled at him. "The captain is right. We need her knowledge of this arctic wilderness." He added almost as an afterthought, "She won't lie if we take her with us. Her survival will depend on ours. And if you'll agree to spare the captain and the exec if she goes with us willingly, we stand a chance of making it out of this icebound hell!"

Henke stared at him, as if surprised at such carefully thought-out planning by a mere naval lieutenant. He slowly lowered the Walther, apparently reluctant to let go of his murderous intent but grudgingly aware that Horst was right. He hadn't quite trusted him enough to give him the pistol or the knife, but his instincts told him the engineer was right in this. He looked at Inga. "Well, Frau Brandt? Come with us willingly, giving freely of your expertise and yourself," he couldn't resist a lecherous

165

smirk, "and in exchange I'll leave these two alive. Let them find their way out through the Northwest Passage if they can while we'll be bound for warmer climes. Well?" he persisted impatiently, and raised the pistol menacingly again.

"No!" Werner answered before she could. "Henke, for the last time, don't go out on that ice." He looked at his former chief engineer. "For God's sake, Horst, believe me. Tell him it's suicide. It's—"

"Shutup, Reutemann!" Henke snapped.

Inga was tugging at the captain's sleeve. "It's all right, Werner, I'll do it. I'll go. It's the only way. Otherwise he'll kill the three of us." Turning slightly away from the general so that she faced only Werner and Hans, she whispered fiercely, "Let me go. This way there is a chance. Look at the barrier sea ice where he's landing. It's not old, dirty shore ice. It's not land at all! It's an ice pan and a large one. It's not Victoria Island. You'll be able to circle around it. By the time you reach the other side, Henke will be so grateful to see you and find he's not stranded he'll probably kiss you. And they haven't thought to ice the runners on the crate-sleds, and I'm not going to tell them. The ice will build up a drag, slowing them down. So please, Werner—"

"I'm waiting for your answer, Frau Brandt," Henke called impatiently. "You've had enough time for parting words."

She turned. "I'm coming with you, Herr General," she said, pulling away from Werner's reluctant arms.

Werner Reutemann let her go. He watched her walk back into the horseshoe of the bridge, back into Henke's clutches. He knew there was no other way. He knew if he acted now he would be killed and that would be the end of it for him. But he knew too that if Inga or any of them was to have any chance at all, he had to stay alive too, he or Hans. They were the only ones with even the barest chance now of getting the boat through.

But if Inga was wrong about this being just a big floating ice pan and not Victoria Island, Gott en Himmel, he thought, she's got to be right. He watched while Henke had the two loaded crate-sleds dragged ashore across the gangplank, where two ropes for pulling were stretched out in front of each one.

As for General Wilhelm Henke himself, he had thought briefly of forcing several more of the crew to go along to pull the crate-sleds but decided against it. They'd be traveling close and having problems enough with the ice and the elements without having to guard prisoners that would turn on them at the first chance. Better to have the crates pulled by those who thought they too would be sharing in their contents.

He was watching Horst giving orders to two of the sailors, making sure the supplies were secured tightly to the top of each crate. Time enough to settle with him later too, he thought; because once they were all safely into the Canadian provinces, he could always bury the crates and return at his leisure. As for the woman . . .

Still standing in the railed well abaft the bridge with Hans, Werner watched the mutineers cross the gangplank. He made one last try to dissuade Henke. "Think what you're doing, General," he called down. "You're leaving the only shelter in hundreds of miles. You won't have any heaters out on that ice. What happens when a storm hits?" But Henke had already turned his back, and Werner turned to his former chief. "Horst, what then?"

"We'll have the tarp!" Horst call back to him. "We'll rig

it over the crates and crawl between them!" But he suddenly looked anxiously at the general. "He's right about the heat. What'll we do for warmth and cooking a hot meal? There's no fuel out on that ice."

Henke merely looked at Inga. "Your first challenge, Frau Brandt. What do the Eskimos do for heat?"

"Seal oil," Inga answered. "They carry little cooking lamps or stoves, and they burn seal oil. You'd have to kill a seal first."

"So we'll kill a seal," Henke said. "And Horst can rig a stove out of an empty food tin. We'll survive."

Werner was still staring down at Horst. He had given up on Henke. "Stay with the boat, Horst. Tell him your only chance is to stay with the boat."

"Not your boat, Reutemann!" Henke called back. "Your boat is finished, kaput! If you'd taken one of the big new boats like I suggested, things would have been different, but no, you insisted on this old iron coffin. Well, it's going to be your coffin, Reutemann, not mine!"

For an instant Werner wondered if they would all have been better off if he had accepted one of the newer models back in Bergen. But he knew there was no turning back the pages of time. And dammit, he knew Horst knew it too. Why was he doing this?

"Let's go," Henke ordered. "Everything's ready."

The captain and his former chief exchanged one last strained look. Then Horst turned back while two of the mutineers took up the traces on each crate-sled and another got behind each one to push. Henke waved his pistol at Werner and Hans who stood watching silently from the bridge. "Cast off your lines, Kapitän, and wish us luck!"

Werner Reutemann said nothing but stared after them

grimly. Then he stepped to the voicepipe and called down to Jürgen Heuser: "Start the starboard engine, Chief, and hook up the charge."

Standing beside Hans at the coaming, he watched the nine dark figures grow steadily smaller, like burnt-out match sticks against the whiteness of the ice. Two out in front of each crate, hauling it with the traces over their shoulders, and one behind pushing. Ahead of them three more figures, one forlornly smaller as she trudged stubbornly between the other two.

He watched them disappear one by one into a jumble of broken ice slabs and pressure ridges until they had all disappeared. Somehow it was as if the Arctic had suddenly swallowed them. Or as if they had never been.

"Damn, damn, damn." Werner began to pound his gloved fist against the icy steel rim of the coaming. He turned to his exec. "Hans, see if you can get me four volunteers, with spanners and crowbars for weapons."

"K'leu, what—!"

"There are too many ifs, Hans," Werner told him quietly. "I can't take the chance. I've got to go after her."

TWENTY-TWO

Alone on the U-boat bridge, Werner raised his binoculars for the fifth time and glassed the horizon to the northwest, where ominous looking black-bellied clouds loomed against the grayer scud. A needle-sharp wind was in his face, frosting his beard and numbing his cheeks and nose. He turned back toward the south, searching once more among the distant jumble of ice and the narrow cleft in the pressure ridges that only minutes ago had swallowed up Inga and the others. Of all the times for a storm to be developing, he thought.

A low, grinding, grating sound echoed above the idling rumble of the starboard diesel. He lowered the binoculars for an instant, wondering what it was as it stopped and then started up again, more loudly now, echoing all along the portside saddle tanks which were against the bank. When he saw the slack suddenly taken up in the long bowline, he stepped quickly to the voicepipe. "Jürgen, why are we moving?"

"We're not, K'leu," the new chief's voice came back. "Clutch is out. I'm still just topping off the charge."

But the noise continued, and thin edges of the newly-formed ice along the shore broke easily against the U-boat's bulging tanks. The bowline went slack and the sternline suddenly tightened like a fiddlestring as Hans's head and shoulders appeared in the hatchway. He hauled himself out on the bridge.

"They all want to go with you, K'leu, but I've picked four of the toughest, including Haupmann. They're getting supplied now. What's all the noise up here?"

Werner had a worried scowl on his face. "You hear it? I thought the boat was underway, but it's the ice moving."

"Then Inga was right," Hans said. "They're out there on a big ice pan."

"Unless it's just shore ice shifting." Werner was looking back at the approaching clouds again. "And now a storm bearing down on us, a fresh young blizzard in the making. The wind is settling down as if to stay."

A sailor's lean, black-bearded face appeared in the hatch. "Permission to mount the bridge, sir?" It was Chief Petty Officer Bruno Haupmann.

Werner nodded. Haupmann climbed out of the hatch and handed the captain a short crowbar, and then pulled the furred hood of his anorak up over his watchcap. He was followed by three more burly sailors: Obermaschinist Günther Hardegen and the medic, Helmut Kranz, both armed with heavy spanners; and Joachim Lutz, the radio mate, who was flourishing another crowbar.

Lutz also handed up some more of the makeshift snow goggles, along with a bundle of blankets rolled in a tarp. "There's tinned food and metal rods for tent poles rolled up inside too, Herr K'leu," Haupmann reported. "We can weight down the edges with heavy chunks of ice."

They watched while the sailors carried the bundles over the side of the tower and waited down on the casing beside the gangplank, which was rattling and scraping with the movement of the shifting ice.

"Better cast off as soon as we're ashore, Hans," Werner told his exec. "Those lines are going to snap anyway if the strain isn't relieved soon."

Moving to the voicepipe, Hans ordered the duty watch up through the foredeck hatch to stand by the lines. Then he looked around again at Werner. "I still think you should stay with the boat, K'leu. Let me lead the shore party."

Werner shook his head, hefting the crowbar in his mittened hand to test the balance. "No, my friend, you can handle the boat as well as I. And Henke is my problem. I should have dealt with him before this happened. Just try to work around the ice pan clockwise and surface on the south side. If it's too far, or the ice is too thick, or if it isn't an ice pan at all, I'll try to meet you back here," he pushed back his sleeve to see his watch, "in ten hours."

"That's not much time, K'leu."

Werner smiled grimly. "I know, but it's all we can risk, if that much, with a storm coming and an unknown distance to cover, and this constantly shifting ice. At least Henke's party should be moving more slowly than we. If we catch up and get Inga back, that's all we'll try for. We'll abandon the crates. Anyway, ten hours, no more. Then the boat is yours. Resume the voyage." His eyes held his exec's sternly. "That's an order, Hans. You'll have only a skeletal crew, but it'll be enough to get the boat and what's left of the treasure through to Japan."

"Jawohl, K'leu."

"You'd better put something ashore behind us—an empty potato crate maybe—something to mark the spot for both of us if we do have to try and rendezvous back here. Till then, goodbye, Hans, and good luck."

They shook hands. "Luck to both of us, K'leu," Hans said, then Werner turned and climbed down the tower to the deck casing.

Twenty minutes later Werner and Haupmann and the three sailors had reached the cleft in the first pressure ridge where the others had disappeared. They paused to look back. The U-boat, with her ice-sheathed, dazzle-striped camouflage, and long icicles bedecking her rails, deflecting wires fore and aft, was already almost invisible against the stormy sky. She backed slowly away from the shore and turned to start her clockwise probe.

The place where she had been was marked now by a crate left on the ice, a crate already only barely visible. Hans had thoughtfully stuck a long metal rod upright through its top. An oily black rag was tied like a flag to its tip and was already stiffening in the freezing northwest wind as blowing ice particles added to the rapidly deteriorating visibility.

Someone—most likely Hans—waved from the U-boat's bridge, and Werner waved back. Then he turned, and motioning the others to follow, he led the way through the narrow cleft in the pressure ridge and out across the flatter ice on the other side.

Sometime later it began to snow. With the light dusting of snow on the ice, the crate-sled runners and footprints ahead of them were leaving a clear enough trail, except in places where the hard ice had been swept clean by the wind.

The broad ice pan was not as smooth as he'd expected. It was covered with small mountains of jumbled, jagged sea ice, with crazily tilted slabs taller than a man. Great pressure ridges and rounded hummocks continuously blocked his view of the terrain immediately ahead so that he had only the tracks to follow. Even they were continuously weaving back and forth as Henke's party worked its way through the same clutter of ice.

Werner, glancing behind him at the others, wondered if they thought he was mad too, bringing them out here on the ice with spanners and crowbars to go against Henke's two guns.

Surprise, that was his only plan. But could he even hope to surprise them? They could as easily lie in wait and surprise him, if they thought he might be following. And could he even catch up with them? There was no sign that they were slowing down; no sign that the runners might be loading up with ice as Inga had predicted. If he suddenly climbed through the next clutch of broken ice and there they were, what in hell would he do? Throw his crowbar at them?

Their boots made faint squeaking sounds on the ice as they moved. Behind their backs the wind was picking up, beginning to gust. The snow was swirling thicker and faster, beginning slowly to fill in the tracks ahead.

Anxiously, Werner glanced back at Haupmann's stern, determined features peering out of his hood. He began to increase the pace, shifting the crowbar to his left hand and clenching and unclenching his right to restore the circulation. Vaguely, his numbing brain wondered how long it would take for their feet to freeze.

TWENTY-THREE

Trudging woodenly between General Henke and Leutnant Wolff, her mittened hands thrust deep in the pockets of her anorak and her back hunched against the bitter wind, Inga Brandt tried to collect her own numbing thoughts and focus on what was happening around her.

They were making surprisingly good time in spite of the runners icing up and the obviously deepening weariness of the six men pulling and pushing the heavy crate-sleds. But nothing seemed to satisfy Henke, who grumbled and stamped his boots and sipped at his flask at every rest stop, and who constantly urged them to greater speeds.

They had stopped again, dogged by increasingly poor visibility due to the light snowfall and frequent heavy gusts of wind. Inga began to wonder just how large this ice pan really was, and whether Werner would be able to work his submarine around it to meet them on the other side.

She even wondered if she should mention the plan to Henke, but instantly dismissed the thought. The general wasn't discouraged enough yet to take that kind of news as a blessing. She glanced over uncertainly at the SS officer and Horst, who were holding a mumbled council by themselves while the six sailors sat miserably on the crate-sleds, resting and hugging themselves in a vain attempt to keep warm.

"All right, all right," Henke muttered moments later, gesturing impatiently, "but let's get moving. We've got to get more miles behind us before we're forced to stop and rig a shelter from this storm."

Then, while the sailors picked up the traces again and the general turned and relieved himself against a low hummock of ice, Horst Wolff walked over to Inga. Bending, he pulled the mitten off his good hand with his teeth and tucked it under his arm while he pretended to tighten his boot and whispered, "Keep your eyes on me, Frau Brandt, and be ready to move quickly. When we climb through the next pressure ridge I'm going to try for Henke's gun."

"What—?" Inga stared down at him, bewildered. But he only straightened and continued talking as he pushed his hand back in his mitten. "You and I are going to head back and chance it that the boat is still around." He nodded toward Henke and the others. "I don't think they'll leave their precious treasure just to overtake us."

"But," she started. But Horst had already turned away as Henke rejoined them, and the sailors got the crate-sleds under way again.

Walking between them once more, Inga tried to sort out what Horst had just told her. What had he meant? Was he really turning against Henke now? Going back to find the boat? But the boat wouldn't be there! She glanced up at the tall lieutenant and almost said it aloud.

Ahead was a formidable jumble of ice. Henke was already heading for a low, wide gap that looked like an easy way through. Inga was so caught up in the confusion of how she was going to get a chance to tell Horst that they were on a huge ice pan instead of Victoria Island, and that Werner was trying to work the boat around to meet them, that she didn't notice the gradual slant of the ice under their feet or the wide, gray depression just beyond the gap in the pressure ridge.

Behind them the six men moving the crate-sleds noticed the steady decline with obvious relief as their heavy loads seemed suddenly lighter and slid more easily, even gaining speed as the slant of the ice increased. Henke was already through the gap, shouting, "C'mon, this way!"

"Wait!" Inga shouted. The sudden horror of what they were approaching belatedly jarred her senses. But even Horst was pulling her forward now, as the three of them had to run to keep ahead of the on-rushing crates. As they went through the gap, Inga was still pleading for them to stop. She felt the slight heaving of the ice under them and know it was too late.

Henke, screaming in sudden terror, veered away to the left as Inga and Horst scrambled off to the right, hand in hand, while the sight and sounds of cracking ice streaked away in all directions and split the air like gunshots.

The crate-sled immediately behind them wasn't quite so fortunate. Meyer and Godt, who were hauling on the traces, dropped them immediately, but then, foolishly, turned around to try and halt the heavy sled. The incline was too steep and the sled's momentum too great. Meyer managed to leap clear on one side at the last moment, but Godt was knocked flat. He went sliding on his back only to disappear with a shriek into the widening patch of black water, followed immediately by the crate-sled which by then had overrun its traces. One of the ropes was tangled in the legs of Kern who had been pushing. He too was dragged into the black water, his final scream cut off as if by a knife.

A great gout of air emerged from the circular hole, followed by a shower of iridescent bubbles. Then there was nothing, just the cracked ice surrounding the melt. The hole bobbed with dozens of fragments of ice.

Already a frail spider-web tracery of new ice was starting to reform on the dark surface as the others stood around in shocked silence, stunned and incredulous at how quickly and effectively the Arctic could mete out death.

Meyer, the surviving sailor from the first sled, stood beside Henke, shaking not wholly from the cold, still not quite believing he had escaped while his mates had died. The general himself seemed speechless and simply stared, first across the melt at Inga and Horst, then at Berchtold, Schulz, and Schmidt who had managed to stop the second crate-sled safely in the gap before disaster overtook them too.

Inga found herself gripping Horst's arm and trying not to blame herself for the deaths of the two men, though she knew she was to blame. She should have seen the melt in time to warn them but she hadn't. The fact that they were mutineers and a party to her being held hostage by Henke didn't seem to lessen her responsibility.

The general, recovering from his own shock, seemed to be more concerned now over the loss of the treasure crate. He too blamed Inga. He had found his voice and was delivering a stream of curses that made her glad the wide melt was still between them.

Horst seemed to appreciate the wide melt too. "I think we'd better make our break now, Frau Brandt," the big engineer said, "gun or no gun. If we can get back through the gap in this pressure ridge, I don't think any of them will be in any shape or mood to follow us."

"We can't go back," Inga told him swiftly. "The U-boat won't be there." She looked up and met his clear gray eyes. "This isn't Victoria Island, Herr Leutnant, it's just a large ice pan with a melt in the middle of it. Werner's trying to work the boat around to meet us on the other side."

Horst Wolff's eyes crinkled and his sudden laughter was outrageous. "Gott en Himmel!" he roared. "The K'leu's a fox. I wondered why he gave you up so easily."

But Inga wasn't smiling. She was pointing across the melt at General Henke who had drawn his Walther pistol.

TWENTY-FOUR

Through Werner's binoculars it had all seemed to happen almost in slow motion.

Desperate now to catch up with Henke's party before the snowfall covered their tracks, he had left Haupmann and the others resting in the lee of a massive ice hummock while he struggled to the top. There he had first looked for some sign that it really was just a big ice pan they were crossing. But with the blowing snow and low clouds, visibility was only a few hundred meters in any direction.

Then, still sprawled on his belly with the slitted leather goggles pushed up on his forehead and the binoculars surveying the ice immediately ahead, he had spotted the tiny figures and the two crate-sleds just starting through a wide gap in a pressure ridge. He was about to lower the glasses and call down to Haupmann and the others when the figures suddenly split apart, one veering to the left and the other two to the right, the three of them apparently trying to avoid a broad, grayish area directly in front of them. He saw too that they were successful, while the crate-sled behind them plowed straight on, evidently unable to stop, and then disappeared through a sudden opening in the ice, taking two of the sailors with it.

Half sliding, half falling back down the side of the

hummock to the bottom where the others were waiting, Werner told them what he had seen.

"So that leaves Henke with only the girl and five men," Haupmann said. "An almost even match except for the guns."

"That's why we've still got to have surprise on our side," Werner told him. "I doubt if they're watching behind them, but they might be. Horst Wolff might think of it. So we'll make our approach from wide to the left and use the broken ice slabs and hummocks to keep out of sight until we reach the ridge itself. Then we'll move close along this side of it to the gap. I'm gambling that with the storm continuing, they'll take a rest now to consider their losses. But we'll have to move quickly. If they keep moving, and this snow keeps falling, there soon won't be any tracks to follow."

"And what about Hans and the boat, K'leu? Any sign of it from the top of that hummock?" They were all stamping their boots on the ice and huddling close, trying to drive out the numbness. "Or even of another side to this island?"

Werner met the petty officer's frankly worried gaze. "No, Bruno. No sign of either one. It must be a very large ice pan."

If it's an ice pan at all, Werner was thinking. Inga could be wrong, but no use worrying the others about that now. They would get Inga first. Then he would have to decide if they should reverse their course and risk trying to get back to the original landing point in the hope that Hans would return there too. It had been nearly three hours since they had left.

On the other side of the pressure ridge, Inga was more certain than ever that they were on an ice pan. A huge one, to be sure, but if the melt was near its center then they were half way across. She had told Henke as much, as well as the fact that their only chance now was to reach the other side and Werner's U-boat. "And he certainly won't take you aboard if I'm not alive and well," she had added defiantly.

Reluctantly, the SS general had put away his gun. He was still frustrated and angry, but glum now too and enervated. Appalled by the sudden loss of half the loot and exhausted by even this short dash across the ice, he didn't really know what to do. They couldn't have gone more than five or six miles. He allowed Horst and the four surviving sailors to rig a shelter by draping the tarpaulin over the remaining crate, locating it close against the lee side of the pressure ridge and well away from the awful depression in the ice. Then they all huddled together inside and listened as the still gusting wind swung around to the northeast.

But even under the lee of the ridge the stiff tarp rattled and shook around them as Horst, working by the yellow glow of a flashlight, tugged off his mitten with his teeth and dug out a bar of nearly frozen chocolate which Inga broke into fairly even pieces before passing it around.

Henke accepted his share wordlessly, then slipped it into his mouth and asked Horst, "You think she's telling the truth, Leutnant?"

The engineer glanced at Inga and nodded. "What has she to gain by lying? We will find out eventually. And besides, it is like the captain. It is what he would do. He would not really give her up. He is full of surprises. It is the only reason we survived the war aboard that boat, Herr General, having a resourceful captain."

None of them said anything for awhile, then Henke

made another decision. "We will wait out this storm, then try to find the sub," he said. "I will bargain with Reutemann as an honorable man, our lives for hers. But we will keep the guns and the treasure."

"That wouldn't be wise, General," Inga told him carefully, glancing at Horst and hoping for his support. "Waiting, I mean. The storm may grow worse. It could last for days. Without a fire for warmth we will soon freeze. And the ice conditions are constantly changing. Werner can't keep the boat on the surface for long. We should keep moving, abandon this second crate, and—"

"No!" Henke barked venomously. "No. We will take the treasure crate!"

"Verflucht!" Horst swore disgustedly. "There are six more crates on the boat, and the men are already exhausted. We'll be lucky to get ourselves back."

"We are with you, Leutnant," Berchtold spoke up glumly. "The crate has been getting harder to move with every step. It's not worth it."

They all stared at Henke who was nervously rubbing his bare hands together for warmth. He was a man alone, and he knew it. The group's physical isolation in the desolate Arctic was bad enough, without the added psychological burden of personal isolation from the group, and he felt it strongly. His eyes betrayed his immense fatigue, as well as the fears and tensions of his failure. "All right," he relented at last, "five minutes more rest, then we'll leave the crate behind and try to find the damned U-boat."

TWENTY-FIVE

The great white bear, shuffling and snuffling along with her two cubs, was moving with a deceptively ungainly gait, her three-inch long claws clattering against the ice. She was hungry, and her hunger had put her in such an exceptionally ugly mood that she even snarled and cuffed at the cubs when she suddenly changed course and they got in her way.

Though on the ice pan she wasn't stranded, having swam over from the mainland only the day before while hunting seals. But so far it had not been a successful hunt, and the pangs in her belly had driven her relentlessly on, until her keen nose had suddenly caught a vaguely familiar scent on the northeast wind.

Rearing up on her hind legs, she startled the cubs by stretching to her full six and one-half feet, pawing the air and growling as she sniffed the wind. Because the scent stirred oddly unpleasant memories as well as a promise of a meal, she growled again and whined ominously. She clicked her long yellow teeth as she lowered herself again to all fours, her thousand pounds jarring the ice as she lumbered forward at an even faster pace.

Werner Reutemann's party, working its way along the windward side of the pressure ridge, cautiously approached the gap. The snow was falling heavily now, hurled against their backs by the wind, and the captain knew the time factor was getting critical. It might already be too late to find Hans and the boat again, even if he could safely free Inga.

He stopped abruptly, spotting the wide gap in the ridge just ahead. Turning, he motioned to the others who drew close around him. "Bruno." Werner didn't want to raise his voice above the wind now, so he cupped a mittened hand to the petty officer's ear. "Let's you and me see if we can climb the ridge and look over on the other side."

Haupmann nodded and signaled the others to stay where they were. Then he and Werner began climbing the rough, sloping sides of the ice ridge. Struggling to the top, they bellied down and stared at the scene below.

The crate-sled was obviously being abandoned. Henke was directing his men in rolling up their tarp and bundling their blankets into packs to carry their food. Inga and Horst Wolff were standing off to one side, watching.

Haupmann, shifting his spanner to his right hand, whispered, "Now, K'leu?"

"Not yet." Werner was watching Henke's men hoist the bundles and the tarp onto each other's shoulders and then set out, grouped behind the general and Horst. Inga had been put in front to lead the way, probably to spot any more melts.

"Now," Werner said. He glanced back down the ridge and waved to the others to proceed on through the gap. He nodded to Haupmann, "Let's go." And gripping his crowbar he started groping his way down off the ice ridge on the lee side, his petty officer close at his heels.

They reached the flat ice at about the same time that their three men rounded the ridge through the gap.

Together the five of them rushed through the thickening snowfall, their rubber seaboots padding soundlessly now across the snow as they trotted past the abandoned crate-sled.

None of Henke's group had even glanced back. When a tangle of broken ice cakes loomed ahead, it looked like a perfect ambush site. Tremendous pressures had forced the ice upwards in a twisted, tortured, volcanic like upheaval which presented a massive frozen fantasy of myriad forms. But there was only one problem. Henke's party, no longer burdened with the crate-sleds, was traveling almost as fast now as Werner's, and the captain knew he could never hope to circle around in time to take advantage of the tumbled ice. He knew he simply had to overtake them now, from behind. He signaled Haupmann and the others to increase their pace and close the distance.

Then, at the last moment, though no sounds rose above the moaning wind, one of Henke's men looked back and immediately cried out a warning.

Another of Henke's men turned then and drew a gun. But in a blur of motion and confusion Horst Wolff leaped forward and knocked down the sailor's arm so that the echoing shot went into the ice. He was too far away to do anything about Henke who, with a look of incredulous alarm, had also drawn his pistol with murderous intent.

Inga was the one who moved toward the general, but she slipped and fell on the ice as Henke took careful aim at the U-boat captain. Horst stepped in front of Werner just as the general squeezed off the shot.

As Horst fell, Haupmann reached Henke with his spanner and the crack of a breaking bone in the general's arm could be heard even above the storm as his gun flew from his hand and clattered on the ice. The rest of Henke's men had no fight left in them, and the brief skirmish was ended as Haupmann picked up both guns and moved to where Werner and Inga were kneeling beside the gravely wounded engineer.

Cradling Horst's head on his arm, Werner tried to staunch the flow of blood that was already seeping through his clothes and congealing in the cold, but the engineer shook his head. "No time for that, K'leu," he whispered hoarsely. A pink froth bubbled up to freeze on his lips. Something deep inside him gurgled ominously.

"Why? Why, Horst?" Werner whispered in anguish. "You damned fool. I never believed you'd really turn on me."

"I found," Horst grasped the hood of the captain's anorak and pulled his face closer, "I found out Henke was quietly recruiting mutineers among the crew. He even approached me, and I went along to find out the plan." He paused, breathing in rasping gasps. "I started to tell you, but the emergency dive took all our attention. Afterwards, as we rode the undersea current, I should have told you then, but I thought I could trap him. Then, when you discovered the missing chart," Horst grimaced with pain and shook his head, "Henke acted prematurely and surprised me too. I had to go along to keep him from killing us all. Mein Gott, K'leu, you—we—" He gagged. His head fell back and his eyes glazed over as he stiffened in Werner's arms. Then his grip relaxed, his breath came in one long, sighing gasp. His head lolled over as his life left him.

Werner felt for a pulse, knowing he would find none. He stared up at Inga, his eyes blurred. Only for some reason the woman bending over them wasn't Inga, it was

Gerda, his dead wife. As he stood again, mixed emotions fought within him, deep rage and bitter sorrow. At last a terrible disappointment and despair took over at this final predicament. Because he now no longer believed they would find the U-boat again. The ice pan was too large.

Inga put a hand on his arm. "Werner," she whispered anxiously.

But the captain only looked around at Haupmann and his own three sailors who were standing guard over Henke and his four. The SS general was sullenly silent as he held his broken arm with his face contorted in pain.

"I ought to kill you now," Werner told him coldly, including the others in his hard gaze. "All of you."

But Inga's hand was suddenly gripping his arm tightly, and her tautly repeated, "Werner! Werner!" had a strange, shrill note of near hysteria. He was momentarily puzzled by the sheer naked terror in her eyes. She appeared actually paralyzed with fear. He followed her gaze beyond Haupmann and Henke and the others and saw its horrendous cause.

Out of the jumbled confusion of ice behind them, emerging from the tumbled eruption of frozen columns and slabs like a specter out of the storm, and rearing up on its hind legs as it rushed them with a roar, was one of the largest, most dangerous and unpredictable carnivors in the world.

TWENTY-SIX

For an awful moment they all stood motionless in a kind of mindless shock, their limbs leaden, their mouths gone dry and gaping. Then the moment was gone and the adrenalin soared as thought and movement returned.

Berchtold, one of Henke's men, was the first to turn and run. But he was also closest to the great, gnashing white horror that was bearing down on them. He took only two steps before one of the huge clawed forepaws caught him across the small of his back, crushing his spine as it lifted him and sent him in a pinwheeling skid across the ice.

General Henke was next in line, but he reacted with surprising speed, grabbing Inga with his good arm and shoving her into the bear's path. But Werner was quicker, moving in a diving roll that carried both himself and Inga out of the charging-animal's reach and leaving Henke square in its way as the others scattered in all directions.

The bear was not choosy. She was merely hungry and angry, and not a little confused and frightened herself at finding so many of the two-legged creatures she knew as man. Having deposited her two cubs safely in the jumbled ice before her attack, she had rushed out on the flat and found a larger party than she had expected. Since she still carried on her thick hide the scar of her one previous encounter with man, when a high-powered rifle bullet had seared through her massive left flank, it caused her to pause, the memory still painfully clear.

But the man's death and the taste of his flesh were even more vivid. So now, having crushed the spine of one of these men, and missing two more that were almost under her, she saw the others scattering. Only one was still within reach, and she took him with all the fury and hunger and fear left in her

Wilhelm Henke's piteous shriek was cut off in midair as the bear eviscerated him with one blow, her great clawed paw spilling his guts out on the ice. In that instant Henke was reduced to a bright crimson smear. Roaring and snarling and whining in her fury, her teeth and claws rended cloth and flesh alike, crushing bones and flagellating the remains until the SS general was nothing but a bloody bag of rags.

Werner and Inga and the others, having gathered again some distance away, were watching in grim horror and morbid fascination when the bear suddenly left Henke and went loping over to Berchtold's body, which she began mauling and mutilating savagely too. Werner, crouching, could hear Inga retching beside him. Haupmann's horrified whisper was close to his ear. "K'leu, won't it come after us now?"

Werner stared at him, then looked around at the others. "I don't know."

"Look," one of the men was pointing. The bear had turned and was climbing back into the jumble of ice leaving blood-reddened tracks on the snow behind her. Moments later she emerged with her two cubs in tow. Rearing tall, she roared and pawed the air defiantly before coming down with her forepaws on the ice so hard they could feel the vibration under them.

The cubs began stalking Berchtold's body playfully but cautiously while the old bear grunted and snuffled and growled, sniffing the wind suspiciously again since her poor eyesight had lost track of her enemies. But the wind was against her now. She moved quickly back to Henke's corpse, which was only a sticky-red, misshapen lump that gleamed in stark contrast to the whiteness of the ice. There she began to feed.

"We'd better go, K'leu," Haupmann whispered anxiously, "while she's busy."

Werner looked at him. "Go where?"

"Where?" Then he understood. Ahead of them now was the bear.

Werner was helping Inga to her feet, turning her away from the grisly scene. "The ice pan is too large anyway," he told Haupmann. "We can only turn back, and hope that Hans and the boat have returned to the original landing point too."

They hurried now, even though Werner tried to pace them. There weren't but a few hours left. He knew that if he had guessed wrong—if Hans hadn't realized the pan was too large and turned back too—then he had signed their death warrants as surely as if he had led them right into the path of the bear.

Inga soon seemed to be having trouble keeping up, and Werner motioned the others on while he half carried her over the ice until Haupmann too dropped back and came alongside to help. The storm was worsening, the wind settling in with a steady mindless wail that was nearing gail force. Visibility was only a hundred meters at best now.

"We're going to have to stop, K'leu!" Haupmann

shouted. "Set up some kind of shelter! We'll only get lost or frozen in this!"

Werner nodded but pressed on, guided only by instinct now. It was getting colder and he knew Haupmann was right. He was beginning to sweat, and to sweat in arctic temperatures was to freeze. But the thought kept needling at the back of his mind, Had they put enough distance between themselves and the bear? Would feeding off the bodies of Henke and Berchtold satisfy her? Or only whet her appetite for more?

Then he remembered something else and stopped. Horst's body was back there too.

He was holding Inga erect and looking back as Haupmann called ahead for the others to stop.

"K'leu?" the petty officer waited for orders.

"Horst." Werner spoke the name so low that Haupmann could only read his lips.

"Horst is dead, K'leu!"

"But his body is back there with the others. The bear—"

"There is nothing we can do for Horst now, K'leu." Glancing ahead toward the others, he saw that they had found and grouped around the abandoned crate-sled near the gap in the ridge, though the ridge itself was barely visible in the storm.

"Come on, K'leu," Haupmann urged him, "we're back at the pressure ridge. The crate is just ahead. We can make our shelter around it. K'leu!" he shook the captain's arm. "Think of Frau Brandt, K'leu, she is near exhaustion!"

Werner nodded. Turning, he lifted Inga in his arms and carried her the last remaining meters to the crate where the others were already throwing down their bundles and spreading the heavy tarp. Rigging it over and around the crate, they anchored its top and edges with heavy chunks of ice.

As they raised one side and crawled into the cavelike interior, Werner glanced up and saw the pressure ridge itself disappear in a world of white and strangely muffled sound. Then they were all sitting in the darkness beneath the tarp, settling against the sides of the crate and listening to the ominously rising note of the storm just beyond the stiff, cold canvas walls.

It was a full gale now. Werner thought gloomily, a whiteout. Someone dug a flashlight out of a blanket bundle and turned it on. Haupmann brought out two frozen chocolate bars, broke them into nine fairly equal bits, and passed them around.

Werner had to coax Inga to taste hers. Her eyes in the flashlight glow were sunk deep in the dark hollows of her face. She stared almost through him as she mouthed the icy sweet in silence. He could see only defeat and despair in those green eyes now, not even an inkling of hope. He wondered bitterly how much her eyes reflected his own.

Because it was on the faces of the others too, as Werner looked around in the dull yellow glow of the shielded light. They who had looked on him almost as a god aboard his U-boat knew he was completely out of his element now. Here on the ice he was as helpless as any of them, and he knew they sensed it.

Inga of course, had more knowledge of their real situation than any of them, and Werner sighed heavily. He still felt they might have made it. Hans still might make it. Pulling back his sleeve, he held out his watch to the flashlight glow. Almost seven hours now, and his orders were to resume the voyage if they hadn't regained contact within ten.

When they had passed the blankets around and

everyone seemed as comfortable as conditions would permit, Werner told them to switch off the light to save the batteries. They sat there in the cold darkness, temporarily safe from the raging elements without. But Werner's mind kept drifting back to Horst's body out there on the ice.

They were all startled by the sudden alien sound that cut through the howling storm like a knife, a brief, shrill, unearthly sound, distorted by the wind. Someone switched on the light again and their shadows leaped up starkly around them. A light fog from their breaths hung close under the ceiling of the tarp as Werner looked at the others. From their wary, questioning glances it was obvious he had not imagined it.

Then rustling, clattering sounds could be heard just outside. A corner of the tarp was tugged loose and began to rise ominously. A single, unanimous, unvoiced thought seemed to leap savagely into everyone's mind simultaneously. The great ice bear had followed them!

TWENTY-SEVEN

As a corner of the tarp was raised violently from the outside, two ice-whiskered faces peered in. One belonged to Chief Petty Officer Hermann Schlag, while the other, younger features were those of Maschinistmaat Jon Müller. Müller had a crowbar gripped in his upraised hand, but he lowered it quickly on sighting the captain and grinned through puffed, cracked lips.

Werner and the others could only stare incredulously as the two men from the U-boat crowded in under the tarpaulin and secured it behind them. "How did you get here?" Werner finally managed. "And where is Hans and the boat?"

Schlag had settled wearily into a corner. "Donnerwetter, K'leu, but it's good to get out of that wind." He had removed his mittens and was rubbing and blowing on his hands. "The lieutenant has surfaced the boat in a cove less than a mile east of here, K'leu," he explained. "He judged the ice pan to be too large. And with the ice thickening too in this storm," he shrugged expressively, "he didn't think he could get to the other side in time. There wasn't really time to go back, so he put us ashore in the cove and sent us west to try and cut your tracks." He shook his head. "We barely saw them in time. All that was left were the faint twin traces of those heavy crates, and they were nearly filled with snow. There were no footprints at all."

Haupmann handed the newcomers each a piece of chocolate, which they popped in their mouths gratefully. Schlag, noticing the weakening beam of the flashlight, dug into his coat pocket and produced a candle stub. "Here, save your batteries." He scratched a match on his thumb nail and lit the candle, the tiny flame flickering eerily under the canvas as the flashlight was extinguished. "Müller here let out a Swiss yodel when he saw your camp, to draw you out, but when no one came we weren't sure what we would find inside. I see you got Frau Brandt back, K'leu, but where is the general and Leutnant Wolff, and the other crate-sled?"

Werner explained all that had happened since they'd left the submarine, and when he had finished Schlag whistled softly. "An ice bear, K'leu? You are lucky indeed."

"It's good you found us," Werner told him, "but it may all be for nothing. Even your tracks will be filled in behind you now, and in this storm how are we to find our way back to this cove where Hans is waiting?"

Schlag smiled and nudged Müller. "The lieutenant thought of that, K'leu. We broke up another of the treasure crates and made a bundle of stakes. Müller here donated a pair of his red flannel underwear."

"We staked our way every few feet with a piece of the flannel tied to each one, K'leu," Müller explained proudly.

"Like dropping bread crumbs," Schlag added, "only hopefully your ice bear's not going to eat the stakes."

"Then we've still got a chance," Haupmann breathed more easily.

Werner nodded approvingly. "It seems I left the boat in capable hands."

"But we also found something strange, K'Leu," Schlag added. "When we broke open the crate to make stakes, there was no more treasure—only farm implements."

Werner stared at him, his mind striving for comprehension.

"So the lieutenant had us break open two more, and they both contained heavy machinery parts too, instead of treasure. There were even some bars of just plain lead. The lieutenant cut into them to make sure. And then we opened the last three crates—all the same—machinery and lead bars, no treasure. He said to tell you it's suspicious as hell, that maybe we were never meant to make it safely under the ice to Japan."

Werner looked around at Haupmann and the others, remembering Horst's missing spare parts he was so sure he had loaded. He suddenly wondered if the whole voyage could have been simply a ruse, another deliberate plot to kill Hitler, not save him. His gaze settled on Inga who had been gradually recovering from the experience with the bear. The presence of two new faces from the U-boat seemed to have brought her back to reality, and taking her hands he rubbed them gently as he voiced the question: "Could we all have been duped? Even Henke and the Führer?"

"My God, Werner," Inga whispered, "it has a kind of insane logic, thinking back on it. Maybe they—Bormann, Himmler—who knows?—wanted him out of the way. And when he came up with an ideal plan himself, they naturally went along with it."

Werner thought about it, then shook his head. "But if it was just another form of suicide, why didn't they go along with the first plan to go directly north under the entire polar cap?"

"Because neither you nor anyone else who knew anything at all about the ice would have gone along with that," Inga told him. "This way there was at least a theoretical possibility, however slight, and strongly tempting to try it." She stared challengingly at Werner now. "There still is."

Werner smiled at her returning enthusiasm, and at the supreme ironies of fate. "A fake suicide in the Reichsführerbunker, and a fake escape through the Northwest Passage under the ice. An elaborate ruse within a ruse. A death plot devised around the Führer's own plan for his supposed salvation. And us—all of us—merely pawns in a game of giants."

Taking the crowbar from Müller, Werner twisted around awkwardly and inserted one end of it into a corner of the crate they were leaning against. As he pried loose a board, the cold nails shrieked as they started from their holes. Inside, the dim, flickering candlelight gleamed dully on metal farm tools. Werner dropped the bar in disgust. Then he laughed bitterly. "So Henke was fooled too. He wouldn't have deliberately dragged farm implements across the ice."

"But the real treasure crate, K'leu," Haupmann asked puzzled, "why throw away a fortune like that deliberately?"

"Why? My dear Haupmann, they must have millions more, maybe billions, looted from all over Europe. They could well afford one real treasure crate to allay suspicion." He remembered the crates being loaded in Bergen, and the first one being opened by Kommandant Manfred Voss for Henke to inspect, one picked by Voss himself. What a different game it would have been if Henke had not been in such a hurry and had insisted on opening the other crates. "So we are all scapegoats," he said softly. "The voyage was never intended to succeed." He looked around at the others again, but this time the challenge was in his eyes. "Yet we almost have succeeded. We may still succeed, if we can follow those stakes back to the boat."

"Which we'd better start doing," Inga noted carefully. "These storms can last for days, and even the stakes could soon be buried."

"Then let's go," Werner ordered.

They had rested and even eaten a little. Schlag had said it was less than a mile to the cove. But he still found the coincidence remarkable, that of the eight crates stowed in the torpedo tubes, the one that had broken open and thus initiated Henke's mutiny, had been the one that did contain some treasure. Or had Henke been plotting to try for a mutiny all along? They would never know and it really didn't matter, since even that crate was now gone forever.

Hunched deep in their hooded anoraks and wearing their improvised leather snow goggles, they followed the little red-flagged stakes that kept appearing out of the blizzard a few paces ahead of Schlag and Müller who were leading the way. The cold was brutal now, and Werner kept a tight grip on Inga's mittened hand as the shrill shriek of the wind rose to an insane pitch and gusted right in their faces. Muffled to the eyes with the hoods of their anoraks drawn tight, the icy claws of the wind still sought them out beneath their clothes. Every breath of air was like sucking slivers of glass into their lungs.

The stinging particles clung to their eyebrows, and their

feet and hands were quickly numb again. If this was early summer in the high Arctic, Werner didn't see how even Eskimos survived a winter. It seemed the mile and the little red-flagged stakes would never end. Until suddenly they did.

But Schlag and Müller were standing still as death, and the others gathered quickly, wonderingly, around them. They made out the two stakes left that led to the very edge of the cove. And the shock of it hit them all at the same time. For even with the limited visibility amid the swirling white gusts, it was obvious there was no longer any open water. The cove was iced over and empty. The U-boat was gone.

TWENTY-EIGHT

Rushing to the edge of the cove, several of the sailors knelt on the ice in renewed agony and despair. Ripping off their snow goggles they stared through the swirling flakes at the empty ice-choked area in disbelief.

It was Haupmann who noticed the tiny scrap of paper fastened to the last flagged stake at the very lip of the cove. Removing his mitten he reached down, tore it free, and handed it to Werner.

"'Ice closing in,'" the captain read aloud to the others. "'Am submerging and turning back. Follow shoreline north and will attempt repeated breakthroughs. Hans.'"

"I make it not more than fifteen or twenty minutes ago, K'leu," Schlag said.

"He's right," Inga added. "The ice is newly formed."

Haupmann was stamping his feet and shaking his head wearily. "Twenty minutes or twenty days, we missed him. When the damned ice starts shifting, it waits for no one."

Werner had raised his binoculars and was glassing the ice along the north shore. "Nothing in sight," he said, "though it's hard to tell anything in this storm."

They were all beginning to stamp their feet and clap their sides for warmth now as Werner returned his glasses to their case. "Let's go. We'll find them." But he said it in a hopeful tone he did not really feel as he took Inga's hand.

Strung out in pairs, with Schlag and Müller still leading, they tried to follow the shoreline of the ice pan. It was now getting harder to tell just where the rough barrier ice of the pan ended and the smoother, newer ice began. At least the wind had died down and the snowfall nearly ceased, but the cold remained. Werner felt if they didn't find the boat surfaced soon they would all freeze long before getting back to the original debarkation point, which might be frozen now too.

Still, thinking about it, he didn't regret having gone after Inga. Glancing at her now he attempted a smile of encouragement and squeezed her hand. If it was possible to continue the voyage at all, he knew Hans was as capable as he to do it. For him it was enough now just to be with this woman. He had loved his wife, Gerda, but he knew now his real love then had been the Kriegsmarine. Now for the first time, with his naval career ended, his country broken, his final and evidently suicidal assignment an impossible adventure that just might succeed, he found he had fallen in love, deeply in love. He wanted suddenly to shout it to the others, to the storm, to the whole wild, awesome, magnificent Arctic. He laughed quietly to himself at his foolishness, at the utter irony of life itself.

"What is it, Werner?" Inga was looking up at him quizzically. "You actually look happy."

"I am happy, Liebchen." He hugged her close as they staggered on. "No matter what happens, Inga Brandt, I'm deleriously happy that I found you, my little arctic expert. You are looking at a man in love."

"K'leu!" Schlag suddenly stoppped and shouted.

But they had all heard it, the heavy, booming, cracking

sounds of breaking ice. Then Inga saw it first, not twenty meters from the shore and less than a hundred ahead, the pale, rust-streaked camouflage of a conning tower, thrusting itself up amid a jumble of tumbling ice slabs.

With a shrieking and wrenching of protesting steel against iron-hard ice, a good thirty per cent of the boat's tower had surfaced, clearing the bridge. Werner's small party had already begun to run for it even before the familiar hooded figures emerged from the hatch and waved to them from the coaming.

The railed gun platform abaft the bridge was almost level with the ice, and Werner and Inga waited while the others pushed several broken slabs aside and climbed on board. Hans himself came back into the wintergarten and helped the captain and Inga onto the deck.

"Welcome back, K'leu," Hans said calmly, barely able to restrain his emotions. He was grinning through his beard and gripping the captain's hand warmly. "We missed you."

"Fortunately," Werner answered wryly, "the Arctic postal service is excellent. We got your message."

But Hans was glancing around now and frowning. "This is all of you?"

Werner nodded. "Let's get below and I'll explain." He had noticed the severe but hopefully not crippling damage the boat had sustained in her emergence through the ice: the wintergarten railing bent and twisted like a pretzel, and parts of the icebreaker protecting the bridge sheared clean off. Even one of the periscopes was bent. But they were back on the boat. As the last of them vanished through the hatch ahead of him, Werner, like the others, almost gagged at the familiar U-boat stench coming up from below. It was in violent contrast to the clean fresh air of the past few hours.

But he was also grateful for that same stale environment as he pulled the hatch cover shut over their heads and spun the wheel to dog it. He could hardly believe they had actually made it back safely, though safety was certainly only a relative term in this case.

"Dive," he ordered, dropping off the ladder into the familiar red-dimmed glow of the control room. "Time enough for reunions later. Hans, retain the conn of the boat until I get to know our situation better."

"Aye, aye, K'leu," Hans acknowledged, glancing at Jürgen Heuser, now their chief engineer. "Level off and trim the boat at fifty meters, Chief." Then he called up the tower to the helmsman. "Maintain this heading, Obersteersmann." Stepping to the chart table he showed Werner the plot of their attempted manuever around the ice pan. "Once we've worked our way back to the point of the mutineers' debarkation, K'leu, we can try for another dead reckoning toward McClure Strait. Once we've found that, we can swing southwest and hopefully raise Banks Island and Prince of Wales Sound."

Werner nodded, picking up the pipe he had left on the chart table and sucking the cold stem thoughtfully. "What's our present condition?"

"Seventy per cent charge on the batteries, K'leu, fifty-nine tons of fuel oil, and a ninety per cent charge of compressed air. Propeller packings are leaking again, but they're working on it."

Werner grunted, shrugging out of his anorak. The others had gone to their stations, the surviving former mutineers apparently as eager to resume their duties as their mates. Any punitive measures would have to wait anyway, he thought, until they made port—if they made port. "Why is it so cold in here?" he asked. The interior bulkheads were icy, and it seemed only a little warmer than outside because of the absence of the wind.

"Problems with the heaters, K'leu," Hans explained. "The mechanics are working on them too." He was staring at the captain. "Are you all right, K'leu?"

"Yes, I'm fine," Werner muttered irritably. "It was close, that's all. It's good to be back on the boat. I don't mind telling you, Hans, I felt as helpless as a child out there on that ice." He told him about what happened to the crate-sled and two of Henke's men, about their encounter with the bear that resulted in the general's and Berchtold's grisly deaths, and about Horst Wolff's heroism and loyalty.

"I never believed Horst capable of mutiny anyway, K'leu. I thought it was a touch of arctic madness, like young Karl."

"No, he was only trying to protect us from that fool Henke."

"Well, now I'll confess something, K'leu. I was getting desperate myself to find any of you. The time limit you set was fast approaching, but I don't know if I could have done it, actually left you behind."

"You would have, Hans, as I would have, had conditions been reversed."

"I suppose, but I'm afraid I bent the main periscope breaking through the ice. It was too thick. But like I said, I was getting desperate and there was no other way. I'd already tried the last two torpedoes, but they were both duds. They thudded harmlessly against the ice and sank to the bottom unexploded."

"Well, we've still got the attack periscope," Werner said, and he glanced at the chronometer on the bulkhead and then back at the chart. "We're still making three knots?"

"Jawohl, K'leu."

"Then we should be getting close to where we disembarked. I'll take over now."

"Your pardon, K'leu, but shouldn't you get some sleep?"

Werner smiled wearily. "Have you, exec?"

"No, K'leu."

"Who's on the inverted fathometer?"

"Otto Dietrich. Oder's nerves are shot. We had to sedate him."

"Yes, well, we'll just have to—"

"Open water above us, K'leu," Dietrich reported as if on cue. "A narrow channel. We're losing it."

Hans glanced at Werner who shook his head. "Let it go," he said slowly. "There'll be another, bigger one." And then he added hopefully, "There'd better be."

But a full hour passed before another lead appeared. This time Werner ordered Jürgen to surface, and at least this one was wide and long.

Out on the open bridge the day was hazy but bright, the storm gone. And best of all there were patches of clear sky, and the sun was a pale but distinct glow a few degrees above the horizon. "Hans!" Werner called down the open hatch as the port diesel coughed and roared. The lookouts took their places at the coaming around him. "Send up the sextant fast! We've got the sun and the moon too! And Venus!"

Moments later Bruno Haupmann's whiskered features appeared in the hatchway and he handed up the instrument. Werner, taking a sight first on the fuzzy orb of the sun, carefully adjusted the knobs and dials. "There's only one problem, Bruno," he noted somberly as the petty officer waited in the open hatch.

"What's that, K'leu?"

"These celestial bodies, if we're headed in the direction we think we are, are in the wrong part of the sky."

TWENTY-NINE

"Seventy-four fifteen North. One-twelve twenty West." Werner repeated the latitude and longitude and bent over the chart table in the control room to watch while his exec once again consulted the tables and then replotted their position with the dividers and parallel rules.

Finished, Hans looked up at the captain in astonishment. Each time their position lines had formed almost the same precise triangle. "We both get approximately the same readings, K'leu, and they place us off Dundas Peninsula on the north side of Melville Sound, not on the south side. Victoria Island's some eighty miles across the sound to the south!"

"So much for our dead reckoning under the ice," Werner noted, spotting their location with a neat little cross. "We wind up at McClure Strait after all. It's not more than twenty miles ahead."

Back up on the bridge, with the pounding port diesel moving them among the loose floes at eight knots and creating its own fog as its hot exhaust hit the cold air, they both joined Haupmann and the lookouts.

The smaller chunks of ice banged harmlessly against the U-boat's saddle tanks while Werner called down frequent course changes to avoid the larger ice and the bobbing, iron-hard growlers. Gradually the open lead began to narrow as the ice thickened. Then it quickly ran out, with the wide entrance to the strait still some sixteen miles over the bow.

Ordering the clutch let out, Werner left the engine rumbling noisely and called down for Inga to come to the bridge. He handed her the binoculars. "McClure Strait is some sixteen miles directly ahead. What do you think?"

Focusing the heavy glasses, Inga studied the awesome masses of ice covering the entrance to the strait. She then looked at Werner and shook her head. "It's like we suspected, jammed tight with heavy ice as far as we can see, even with these." She handed him back the glasses. "There's everything caught up in there: rafted ice, bergs, whole floes. Maybe it's just too early in the year," she shrugged.

Werner looked over at his exec. "Lay out a course southwest across the sound for Banks Island, Hans," he said. "Then we'll work our way around to Prince of Wales Strait. But if that's jammed up too—"

"It shouldn't be," Inga said encouragingly. "It hasn't got the reputation of McClure. It's just a lot narrower, and shallow too."

"We can crawl along the bottom if we have to," Werner said, "if it's just got some breathing holes overhead." Ordering the helm put over on a west-southwest heading, he got one more navigational fix before taking the boat once again beneath the ice, this time on her starboard motor, the port switchboard panel having given out again.

Haupmann's report was not encouraging as the electrical artificers bent over the panel, cursing softly. "It was that fire, K'leu. The rheostat's and rotors are shot now. If we had spare parts—"

"But we don't," said Werner, wondering if the many missing spare parts had been arranged for too, as a sort of insurance for failure. He clenched his fists, even more determined now to make it. "Keep after it," he said, and turned to Hans. "What about the damned heaters? The instruments will be freezing up." Everyone had put on extra clothing as a thin sheet of ice formed over the bulkheads.

"Still working on them, K'leu. But so far only two have been restored."

"Then restore more. Once the instruments freeze—" He bit off the sentence unfinished. They were doing their best, and the implication was plain: men were a lot more adaptable to the Arctic than machines.

An hour later the sailor on the inverted fathometer reported, "Open water above us, Kapitän."

"Surface," Werner ordered. "Blow forward tanks. Hard rise on bow and stern planes."

Compressed air shrieked into the tanks, but the boat didn't respond like it should. It was rising, but slowly, sluggishly. Werner glared at Jürgen Heuser.

Then a planesman reported, "Stern hydroplane jammed, sir."

"Switch to manual," Jürgen ordered.

"Still jammed, sir."

Someone cursed bitterly.

"Blow the stern tanks," Werner ordered.

Lumbering up onto the surface, the boat rolled uneasily as Jürgen fought to regain the trim. Werner scrambled up the tower ladder and threw open the upper hatch. Hans and the four lookouts of the duty watch emerged on his heels. The boat continued its silent running on the starboard motor amid drifting wisps of fog and small chunks of floating ice. The overcast was thick again, but Werner spotted a wide lead of open water trailing southwesterly. Lowering his glasses he ordered the motor shut off and the port diesel started.

The cough and comforting roar seemed to beat back the threat of the silent white world around them. It rumbled noisely for several minutes, then suddenly stopped, allowing the deafening arctic stillness to close in abruptly again.

Werner stepped to the voicepipe. "Jürgen?"

"Checking, K'leu."

After interminable suspense he reported the bad news. "Port diesel disabled, sir. Those foil bearings finally gave out."

"Scheissdreck!" Werner swore in angry frustration. "Start the starboard engine." He looked at Hans disgustedly.

"Jürgen is a good engineer, K'leu," the exec said softly.

"But he's no Horst, is he? Horst was our miracle worker. He could hold the boat together with spit and boot leather. And that's what we're going to need now, another miracle."

The starboard diesel coughed twice, then roared to life, pounding voluminously as if to make up for its failing mate as Werner ordered ten knots of speed and called down the steering directions to the helmsman.

The fog was thickening. He turned on the radar, knowing if the lead held and he could maintain this speed, they could raise Banks Island in a few more hours and maybe find a relatively safe anchorage where they could lay up and make what repairs they could. At worst they could lie on the shallow bottom close to shore, because he didn't want to dive in deep water again with only the one half-reliable motor and a jammed stern plane.

At that moment Inga appeared in the hatchway with a pot of fresh coffee and a string of mugs. She requested permission to come up.

Werner nodded.

"It's getting colder, K'leu," Hans noted as they passed steaming mugs to the lookouts and kept three for themselves. "And the barometer is falling."

"I know." Werner was watching the slurried sky. "I'd say we're going to get another gale. Gripping his mug with both mittened hands, he eyed the others over the rim as he sipped at the hot brew. "But if we can make it, and Prince of Wales Strait is even relatively ice-free, then I'm convinced this voyage is at least possible. Maybe not by us, but in one of the newer boats, a big Walther for sure. With a trained skipper and crew, and plenty of spare parts, I'm sure that transit of the Northwest Passage is possible in a submarine." Then he added wryly, "Not that anyone but us cares anymore. Strategically speaking, the war is over."

"I'm not so sure about that last bit, K'leu," Hans observed philosophically. "From what I can tell, wars never really end. There's only an armistice, an agreement not to kill for awhile, a pause for rearming and regrouping that may take years, and maybe a shifting of alliances. Then it all starts over again, and in the next one the fact that a submarine can transit the Arctic beneath the pack ice could be strategically invaluable. From a tactical advantage alone—"

"But what the captain is saying, Hans," Inga interrupted quietly, "is that we're not going to make it. Right, Werner? Not us. Not this time. Not in this boat."

Werner Reutemann looked at them both with a deep premonition of real disaster, and with it a nostalgic sense of eternal sadness at all that was and all that might have been. "No," he answered frankly. "I don't think we are."

THIRTY

So it was over. The war, the voyage, everything. Over. These last few hours were simply the sand in the hourglass running out. Werner Reutemann could actually sense their approaching doom, but he refused to give up. As long as they were alive, as long as they could move at all, they might still beat the bastards who had sent them out here to die.

Stooped over the chart table in the control room, he beat his arms against his sides for warmth and flexed his fingers before working out the plot of their estimated position. Out on the bridge Hans and the lookouts stood against the now howling blizzard as visibility deteriorated rapidly to a few meters. They crept along at four knots, feeling their way with the radar while this latest lead continued to narrow inexorably.

The electrical artificers had the port motor switchboard torn completely apart now, and the starboard motor was out, like the port diesel. The starboard diesel alone throbbed monotonously, steadily, faithfully, like an overworked hausfrau.

Ironically, the stern dive plane had been freed and made operable. But without at least one electric motor functioning, operating under the ice was impossible.

Though approaching the hundred-fathom line, they were still a good fifteen miles off Banks Island where they might land or at least lie in the shallows on the bottom until repairs were made or their air gave out. They were trapped on the surface, and once again the ice was rapidly closing.

He had left orders with Hans to watch for any open lead now in any direction. Mostly to keep busy he began recalculating their remaining fuel against their rate of consumption and distance left to travel. Still fifty-seven tons of oil in the bunkers and almost two-thirds of their journey completed. Enough, dammit, he thought bitterly. More than enough. And an eighty per cent charge on the batteries. But without the motors and the damned heaters, enough was too little. Some of the instruments were already icing up.

He became acutely aware that Jürgen and the others in the control room were casting furtive, anxious glances in his direction. Aware too of the decision that was fast approaching: whether to abandon the boat and take their chances on the ice floes, or keep fighting the hopeless breakdowns until they were frozen in solid or crushed.

Well, he had experienced what it was like out on the open ice in a gale, and leaving the control room he began moving through the various compartments where the men not on watch or making repairs on something were bundled in blankets in their bunks and sipping hot coffee laced with schnapps. He had ordered a full ration all around, though he was determined to maintain the discipline of regular watchkeeping right to the end. They were still German sailors, and they had served their country well. They had served him well, most of them.

The cook had even baked a cake of sorts with Long

Live Germany and Werner Reutemann iced across the top. They were playing records on the gramophone and piping it over the intercom. But instead of the rousing martial aires now, they were plaintive folksongs and ballads, the music scratchy and stilted and oddly anachronistic, but the nostalgia somehow deeply satisfying.

Offering each man a word of encouragement and calling each by name as he passed by, Werner accepted their thin smiles of acknowledgement and wondered if they knew he was really telling them goodbye. Behind their bearded, youthful faces their eyes were sunken, hollow, and old. Life in a U-boat had always been an incessant round of fear, suspense, exhaustion and boredom. And these last few weeks, though incredibly different, had been as bad as any during the war. On top of everything else was the relentless, debilitating effects of the arctic cold. Yet in spite of the ice-hard harshness of reality, they could still smile in the face of death, and he was proud to be among them.

Finishing his tour of the boat, he included even the empty, ghostly forward torpedo room. It was here that he finally realized he would soon be joining his comrades in arms at the bottom of the world's oceans. It was where he felt he belonged, where the whole crew belonged. They were all long overdue. He was just sorry to have brought Inga Brandt to such a miserable and undeserved fate.

He was returning to the control room when he found her standing in the passageway outside his quarters. She was wearing her anorak and mittens. She drew him wordlessly into the curtained alcove where she whispered anxiously, "Tell me, Werner, back there on the ice, when you said you loved me—"

"I meant every word of it, Liebchen."

"Oh, Werner, hold me close."

They held each other while the music still wafted through the compartments. A song of love was ending, a song of warm sun and balmy breezes and lovers strolling along the shore of a crystal lake. Combined with the heavy throb of the starboard engine, and the eerie sounds of the wind outside, beating against the conning tower and whining in the deflecting wires, it made no sense at all, yet it stretched their minds and lifted their hearts.

When the song ended and a new one started, the melancholy strains of "Lili Marlene" rang out in all its bitter-sweetness. Piped up to the bridge, the song echoed across the bleak and endless landscape as if from another world, as well it was.

"I'll have to get back to the control room soon," Werner told her, releasing her but still intensely aware of her nearness.

"I know, duty calls." She straightened, her green eyes brightly moist. "But when is our time together, Liebchen? Maybe in the next life?"

Werner shook his head sadly, wonderingly. "Maybe this was our time together, Inga," he said. Sitting down at his tiny desk, he opened the log and made a final entry:

> *2 June, 1815 hrs. Surfaced in sleet and snow and heavy ice floes approximately fifteen miles east-northeast of Banks Island. One diesel still operable but both dynamotors disabled and unable to dive; snorkel not operable in heavy ice. Making for Banks Island where will abandon boat and attempt overland passage to Sachs Harbour, but open leads are few and closing; barometer falling; wind north-northeast, force 5; temperature 29 degrees F. All heaters now inoperable; main vents and steering gear freezing up. Believe transit of Northwest Passage by submarine still feasible with new boat and spare parts and*

God willing.

Once again he was intensely aware of Inga's presence beside his chair. He stopped writing, laying aside his pencil as she removed one mitten and placed her warm hand lovingly over his. He looked up into her face.

"I must look awful," she said.

"You look beautiful."

"I know I smell awful. You have to admit that." She smiled wistfully, still holding his hand.

"We both smell beautiful." They stared at each other longingly. "My God, Inga," he whispered and pressed her hand to his lips. "Auf Wiedersehen."

"Auf Wiedersehen, my love."

EPILOGUE

On April 17, 1964 two young Eskimo seal hunters, far out on the ice southwest of Sacks Harbour with a sled and dog team and modern .22 rifles, witnessed a strange sight. They thought at first it was a whale caught in an iceberg, but as the ghostly gruesome sight drew nearer, drifting out of the fog, they could plainly see what appeared to be the upper deck and conning tower of a submarine. It was locked securely in the grip of the great green berg, with four men standing silently at the corners of the bridge, all of them frozen solid to the surrounding steel and staring out at the white arctic world through empty sockets, their eyes a long-ago gift to the gulls.

The Eskimos knew all that had prevented polar bears from finishing them off were the steep, ice-coated sides of the tower itself and the concave shape of the ice blocking the afterdeck. For several moments they stared, horrified at the specter. Even the dogs growled low in their throats and the hair on their backs bristled.

They looked at each other in wonder, knowing it was a submarine only because just the year before, while visiting one of the dewline stations, they had seen pictures in an American magazine of the great nuclear boats emerging through the ice. But this boat was so small! And a pale, mottled, rust-streaked color instead of black.

They also knew the submarine must have been drifting around in the ice for a long time. If it worked its way any further south with the spring melt, the great green berg would finally release its grip, allowing both the boat and its mysterious occupants to slip at last beneath the waves and plunge into the depths for its final dive. On the other hand, if it swung north again and survived another summer, it would be frozen once again and simply continue its eternal voyage.

The two Eskimos supposed it didn't matter much which happened, certainly not to the men on board. They continued to watch the macabre scene for several minutes until it faded, ghostlike, back into a swirling fog bank and finally disappeared altogether. For a moment they even wondered if they'd really seen anything at all. Then they shifted their rifles to the crooks of their arms, called sharply to the dogs, and resumed their hunting. It would be a good story to tell back at the trading post. They wondered if anyone would believe them.

STARLOG photo guidebook

All Books in This Special Series
- Quality high-gloss paper,
- Big 8¼"x11" page format.
- Rare photos and valuable reference data.
- A must for every science fiction library!
- Available at Waldenbooks, B. Dalton Booksellers and other fine bookstores. Or order directly, using the coupon below.

SPACE ART $8.95
($13 for deluxe)
196 pages, full color

SCIENCE FICTION WEAPONS
$3.95
34 pages, full color

SPACESHIPS $2.95
34 pages, over 100 photos

Latest Releases

TV EPISODE GUIDES
Science Fiction, Adventure and Superheroes $7.95, 96 pages
A complete listing of 12 fabulous science fiction adventure or super-hero series. Each chapter includes (a) complete plot synopses (b) cast and crew lists (c) dozens of rare photos, many in FULL COLOR.

TOYS & MODELS
$3.95, 34 Pages
A photo-filled guide to the fantastic world of toys and games. There's everything from Buck Rogers rocket skates to a mini Robby the Robot! Full-color photos showcase collections spanning four generations.

SPACESHIPS (new enlarged edition)
$7.95, 96 pages
The most popular book in the series has been expanded to three times the pages and updated with dozens of new photos from every movie and TV show that features spaceships-the dream machines! Many in full color.

HEROES $3.95, 34 pages
From Flash Gordon to Luke Skywalker, here is a thrilling photo scrapbook of the most shining heroes in science-fiction movies, TV and literature. Biographies of the men and women who inspire us and bring triumphant cheers from audiences.

FANTASTIC WORLDS $7.95
96 pages, over 200 photos

SPECIAL EFFECTS, VOL. I
$6.95, 96 pages, full color

SPECIAL EFFECTS, VOL. II
$7.95, 96 pages

VILLAINS $3.95
34 pages, full color

ROBOTS $7.95
96 pages, full color

ALIENS $7.95
96 pages, over 200 photos

Send to: STARLOG G... . FA3 475 Park Avenue South New York, NY 10016

Name

Address

City

State   Zip

Add postage to your order:

HEROES............$3.95	FANTASTIC WORLDS	SPACE ART
VILLAINS...........$3.95	................$7.95	Regular Edition.....$8.95
SPACESHIPS I.....$2.95	ROBOTS............$7.95	Deluxe Edition.....$13.00
WEAPONS..........$3.95	Prices for all of the above:	___Regular Edition
TOYS & MODELS...$3.95	___3rd Class.......$1.75	___Deluxe Edition
Prices for all of the above:	___1st Class.......$1.55	___U.S. Book rates
___3rd Class....$1.00 ea.	___Foreign Air.....$2.50	................$2.00 ea.
___1st Class....$1.25 ea.	SPECIAL EFFECTS..$6.95	___U.S. Priority.$2.57 reg.
___Foreign Air..$2.25 ea.	___3rd Class.......$1.50	...........$3.30 deluxe
SPACESHIPS	___1st Class.......$2.00	___Foreign Air...$7.00 reg.
(new enlarged)...$7.95	___Foreign Air.....$5.50	...........$8.50 deluxe
SPECIAL EFFECTS VOL. II		
..................$7.95	total enclosed: $_____	
TV EPISODE GUIDE BOOK	NYS residents add sales tax	
..................$7.95	Please allow 4 to 6 weeks for delivery of 3rd Class mail:	
ALIENS............$7.95	First Class delivery usually takes 2 to 3 weeks.	

ONLY U.S. Australia and New Zealand funds accepted.
Dealers: Inquire for wholesale rates on Photo Guidebooks.
NOTE: Don't want to cut coupon? Write order on separate piece of paper.

HELL ABOVE WATER
By Harry P. McKeever

PRICE: $2.25   LB856
CATEGORY: War

RAF fighter ace Peter Lorraine, was aboard a troop ship in the Mediterranean when it was torpedoed by a German U-boat. By a strange twist of fate, the captain of the U-boat was engaged to Peter's sister. Peter managed to survive in an overcrowded lifeboat and vowed revenge. He soon found himself in the hands of the Vichy French and was imprisoned in North Africa. Freed by American troops, he enjoyed a brief respite when he fell in love with an American girl, but the horrors of war had only just begun. Again flying combat duty over bloody waters, Peter discovered his own personal hell among the clouds.

SEND TO: LEISURE BOOKS
P.O. Box 511, Murry Hill Station
New York, N.Y. 16156

Please send me the following titles:

Quantity	Book Number	Price
_____	_____	_____
_____	_____	_____
_____	_____	_____
_____	_____	_____
_____	_____	_____

In the event we are out of stock on any of your selections, please list alternate titles below.

_____	_____	_____
_____	_____	_____
_____	_____	_____
_____	_____	_____

Postage/Handling _____
I enclose..... _____

FOR U.S. ORDERS, add 75¢ for the first book and 25¢ for each additional book to cover cost of postage and handling. Buy five or more copies and we will pay for shipping. Sorry, no C.O.D.'s.

FOR ORDERS SENT OUTSIDE THE U.S.A., add $1.00 for the first book and 50¢ for each additional book. PAY BY foreign draft or money order drawn on a U.S. bank, payable in U.S. ($) dollars.

☐ Please send me a free catalog.

NAME _____
(Please print)

ADDRESS _____

CITY _____ STATE _____ ZIP _____
Allow Four Weeks for Delivery